ALONE

To Mike

Alistair Newton

ALONE

A Story Of Intimidation, Extortion, & Murder

by

Alistair Newton

"Standing alone takes a great deal of courage. It means you can't be controlled by a need to be with other people all the time, and to seek their approval."

Copyright © 2008 Alistair Newton

Windward Publishing Company
Berkley, Massachusetts 02779

All rights reserved. No part of this publication may be reproduced, stored in a retrieval system or transmitted, in any form, or by any means, electronic, mechanical, recorded, photocopied, or otherwise, without the prior permission of the copyright owner, except by a reviewer who may quote brief passages in a review.

ISBN 13:978-0-9788424-2-0

Printed in the United States of America

Orders: www.alistairnewton.com

"...someone hit me on the head from behind. It hurt but I was still conscious. I turned and looked straight into the menacing coal black eyes of Humberto Rada, and then he hit me again. The last thing I remembered was the whine of the engines as the turbines spooled up and the props chased them to a howling screaming climax."

Chapter One

"When you find rats in your pantry, who do you call, the FBI?"

"No, I suppose you would call an exterminator."

"Right! Well, let me introduce you to the exterminator: William Thackery O'Keefe."

It was one of those cold, damp, murky days in November when the winds shift west-northwest, bringing a cold front sweeping down from the Canadian Arctic. These cold winds had collided with the warmer currents of the Gulf Stream offshore in the Atlantic producing sleet, rain, fog and low scudding clouds. Sailing season was definitely over, and thankfully the boat was in storage. The only thing of positive value for the day was that Connie and I were warm and snug in the visitor's lounge of the South Fork Nursing Home with Willie Monk. The grounds of the home faced south, overlooking the Atlantic Ocean with its turbulent waves crashing on shore, beating the sandy white beaches without mercy and sending salt spray flying into the air. The sea gulls riding the air currents over the sand would rise abruptly to avoid being drenched when each big wave broke, creating an almost comical dance as they struggled against the wind to stay level and aloft.

"Nice ... d ... day ...," said Willie, slurring his words.

"Surely you jest," I said.

"You didn't let him finish," said Connie.

"...f ... for ... s ... sea...gulls," mumbled Willie, drooling from the right side of his mouth.

Connie was right, I had not let Willie finish. It was difficult for me to get used to his slow, labored speech having known him before the stroke. We worked at State Mutual and then we went on our own as insurance investigators. Together we cracked some of the biggest cases in the business and we were in great demand.

One day Willie came to visit me at my place in the sand dunes on the North Fork of Long Island. He liked it there and after my divorce it was about all I had left, that and my sailboat. We were walking on the beach when Willie collapsed. I carried him to the cottage and put him in my grandfather's rocker on the front porch. That was three years ago and now he was learning to walk and talk all over again. For more than a year he was partially paralyzed. Then the doctors changed his therapy and he began to improve. Now he was able to form short sentences and he could even stand for several minutes with the help of a walker.

"It's amazing how sea gulls never seem bothered by bad weather. When I was growing up in Iowa, the birds always stayed on the ground when the weather turned stormy." Connie said.

"Are there sea gulls in Wilson, Iowa?" I asked.

"No, but there are ducks and geese, hawks and pheasant, and…"

'Okay, okay, I give up," I said, raising my hands in surrender.

'No you don't," said Connie. "You're just saying that to keep me from winning. Anyway, these sea gulls seem to thrive on bad weather: sleet, rain, snow, high winds, and fog. Why don't they stay on the ground or in trees in bad weather like other normal birds?"

'The sea gull is not a normal bird," I said. "It's basically a shore bird but it operates out at sea as well as inland. Some ocean birds, like the puffin, spend their entire lives at sea except for short periods when they come ashore to breed."

'I understand spending one's life at sea, William Thackery O'Keefe, and I understand coming ashore to breed! But tell me why sea gulls always circle around each other like that, squawking and fighting? Have you ever noticed? You never see just one sea gull. They're always in a bunch, and when one finds something to eat, all the others chase him and try to make him drop what he has in his mouth." She finished and seemed quite pleased with herself.

'Sea gulls don't make sense unless you understand them," I said trying to contain myself. "They live in flocks, not bunches, and their mouths are called beaks. Gulls are scavengers which means to trick or dupe. They're experts at stealing each other's food."

'So, on one hand they live in flocks and on the other hand, they steal each others' food. Why do they do that?" she said.

'Alone ..." said Willie, a smile on his face, his lower lip quivering. "They don't ... like ... b... being alone."

"You are kidding me? If I were a sea gull I would go somewhere by myself so when I found something to eat, no one would bother me. Doesn't that make more sense?" Connie said.

"Willie's right. Sea gulls are the original groupies of the bird kingdom. They don't like to be alone. Being with others of their own kind is more important than anything else in their lives. That's why you see them out there in the worst weather you can imagine. Even in a forty knot breeze they get out and fly around because they're afraid something might happen and they won't be there to see it," I said.

"So you're saying the drive to socialize is so great in sea gulls that they will risk anything, even sleet, rain, snow, high winds, and fierce competition for food, just to hang around with their buddies," she said.

"Yeah ... you got it ... B, B, Babe," Willie mumbled as the wind howled around the building.

"You have definitely got it, Babe." I echoed Willie's words and winked at Connie. "Understanding sea gull behavior is important. It helps one master the more complex behavior of humans, who are part of the same animal kingdom of which sea gulls are an important, integral, and visible part. For instance, let us take the sexual behavior of ..."

"Okay! Okay, already. That is quite enough, okay?" She said.

"Yeah ... already," echoed Willie. "Okay."

"Whose side are you on, anyway, you old goat?" I said to Willie.

"Her ... hers." He grinned and pointed to Connie.

'Some partner you turned out to be. Some pal. Here I come to visit, bring my best girl, and you try to steal her right out from under my nose. Nice guy!" I said, acting hurt.

Connie leaned over, put her arms around Willie as he sat in his wheel chair and nuzzled his neck just below his right ear. It was a game we played every time we visited and Willie loved it. The doctors said he needed all the human companionship he could get and touchy feely stuff was good. Doc called it skin hunger and said touching was a treatment used by doctors and nurses in Africa to save orphaned babies. When left alone for long periods of time, they wither away and die for lack of love. They call it Kwakiorcor. I don't know about all that, but I do know that Willie thrived on our visits so we did everything we could to make him happy and it seemed to be working. The head nurse said Willie wasn't sick at all. He was just faking it to get attention, and on several occasions he had tried to prove his virility with one or more of the nursing staff.

'He's not dead yet," she said. "That's for sure. Just bend over next to his wheel chair and he'll prove it." Ahh yes, the dangers of being a nurse.

The doctors and nurses paid more attention than usual to Willie because they thought he owned the nursing home. Actually, it was owned in trust for him and I was one of the trustees. Connie Wilson was another trustee and the third one was my attorney, Saul Goldstein. I scored big on a case about two years ago and I used some of the money to make an offer on the nursing home. The offer was accepted by the out-of-state corporation that owned the place, and that was when Willie's therapy was changed and he suddenly began to improve. Friends like Willie don't come along often. We went back a long way and I owed him a lot.

We left Willie and headed back to Connie's place. I told Connie a story about Willie as we traveled the Long Island Expressway into the city.

It was the day we opened the vault of the Paul Revere Mutual Life Insurance Company in Boston and found it empty. We were hired to find who was siphoning funds from the company but someone tipped off the culprits and everything disappeared before we could nail them. It was one of those moments when an investigation could fall apart and no one would win. We never collected our ten percent fee unless we saved the client money or retrieved their lost assets.

So, there we were with an empty safe. Willie turned and looked at the president and board of directors, who were standing there looking agape at the empty vault and he shook his head.

"Who's missin?" he asked.

"Nobody. Everyone is here," said the president.

"Who had access to the vault?" asked Willie.

"Everyone," came the answer.

There were no safeguards. Willie looked at me and I looked at him and we both looked outside at the building across the street where a flock of sea gulls was perched on the roof, waiting for something to happen.

"See dem sea gulls over there, gentlemen?" Willie pointed with his stogie held firmly between two fingers. "They are all standin' around waitin' for somethin' to happen, like maybe a loaf of bread'll fall off a passin' truck, or a restaurant will toss out a fish head, and then you know what they'll all do?"

Everyone shook their heads. I didn't shake mine because I was with Willie and I was supposed to know what he was doing. Only I didn't have a clue, so I just stood there wondering how I was going to make my alimony payment if we didn't get our ten percent commission.

"Well, gentlemen, what dem sea gulls is gonna do," Willie said in his Bronx accent, "is just what you guys is gonna do. They are gonna all jump on it all at once and fight like hell over who is gonna get what and how much and when."

He turned very slowly to the president of the company and punched him hard in the chest with the two fingers he was using to hold the stogie and said, "Mr. O'Malley, your accountants called us on behalf of the stockholders of this mutual company to investigate a continuing loss, and when we get here there ain't no books, the vault is empty, the accountants is fired, and everyone's come to work on time 'cause they're afraid to miss out on the show. Nobody's missin'. Now, from my vast knowledge of human behavior I'd say it's an inside job, wouldn't you?" Willie poked the speechless Mr. O'Malley again hard in the chest.

'And furthermore, I'd say the bad guys is right here, in this room, this very moment!" Another poke. "Now, since we all understand what's goin' on, let's get to the good part. Youse guys can do it the easy way or you can do it the most difficult of ways. My partner here, Mr. O'Keefe, can go call the police and the Insurance

Commissioner and we can have a public dance where everyone's invited, including the press and the stockholders and their mothers and fathers, aunts and uncles, or we can call dat accounting firm back in here, you guys can re-produce the books, and we can settle this in a friendly manner, which includes my ten percent commission for keeping you rats outta jail. Now (Poke, poke) what'll it be?" Poke!

We got the ten percent. The stockholders replaced the president and his board of hoods and I made my alimony payments for the next six months.

"Sea gulls! Yeah, sea gulls is the key," said Willie as we caught a cab to Logan Airport the next day. "Ya gotta understand sea gulls. They're just like people."

Chapter Two

WE were headed for Connie's place in White Plains and when I finished the story, she said, "Sounds like Willie made a wild guess about those people and he was right."

"Willie never made wild guesses. He had several clues which led him to a conclusion. He trusted his gut reactions and his conclusions. Most people don't trust their own instincts. Remember, Willie's not a college graduate and that's why State Mutual let him go when we worked in New York City. They wanted only college grads. It was called 'upgrading the work force' but Willie was better than ten college graduates because he could see things and he could think in ways a college graduate couldn't. He didn't have the disadvantage of an education. He trusted the instincts and abilities God gave him. It wasn't luck with Willie Monk, it was ability. I saw him use his skills many times. He taught me to believe in myself and my own abilities."

"I thought Vietnam taught you that," said Connie.

"Vietnam taught me to survive while believing in nothing."

We rode in silence for a while as I maneuvered up the Cross Island Expressway for a shot at the Throgs Neck Bridge. My plan was to take the Hutchinson River

Parkway to White Plains, where Connie lived in an executive apartment on the top floor of her company's headquarters building. Her job as Vice-President of Compliance and Standards for Daylight Inns, a national chain of hotels, often required her to work round the clock, so the company provided her with free housing to make up for the pressures and weird hours. We'd known each other for about two years and our relationship had grown to be a solid part of our lives. We had been through some tough situations together and things were getting better. It was a comfortable relationship. We were not only lovers but also friends and I had no intention of giving her up.

"It's always fun seeing Willie," said Connie.

"I think he's improving. What do you think?" I asked.

"Yes, but I feel sad for him when I realize what he must have been like, you know, the way you described him before the stroke," she said.

"He doesn't deserve what happened. If it weren't for me, no one would care about him. His ex-wife and kids treat him like a leper and he has no other family. It's tough being alone in this world. I hope that never happens to me," I said.

"I'll make sure it doesn't," said Connie, rubbing my leg.

We came to the Daylight Inns headquarters, a square four story concrete structure with too much glass, a helo pad on the roof, a row of low cut bushes along the front curb, and an American flag flying from a pole stuck in the front of the glass façade. Ahhh, corporate America, and surprise, a "bunch" of sea gulls was perched on the front ledge of the roof. I drove my Caddy around to the back and down a ramp marked 'Executive Parking', punched in Connie's code, watched the gate open, and drove into the executive inner sanctum.

"Stay with me, Bill," Connie said. "We haven't had much time together since the summer."

I couldn't turn that down so I said yes and gave her a long, passionate kiss.

"Let's go upstairs, Tiger. I'm supposed to set an example for the rest of the company, and it just won't do to have the security cameras recording us rollicking in the back seat of your Caddy," she said.

We rode the private elevator up to her fourth floor suite where we made love, ate spaghetti, and relaxed as we watched an old Mastroianni movie in Italian with subtitles.

'This is great, Bill," said Connie. "I miss the time we had sailing together before we put the sailboat up for winter storage. I miss your children too. Maybe we can have them down for dinner sometime."

'That would be great," I said. "Of course their mother will make things difficult but we might manage to negotiate it."

We went to bed, made love again, and fell asleep in each other's arms. Life was never better and I was very content.

Somewhere in the night the telephone disturbed our slumbers. Connie answered it and came back to the bedroom very upset and crying.

"Bill, I'm sorry but I have to leave. My father has

suffered a massive heart attack and I have to go home right away. They don't expect him to make the night. I am really sorry. I hoped we would spend the day together but now I can't," she said.

"It's all right. I'm sorry about your father. Look, I'll drive you to JFK airport," I said.

"No need, the corporate jet is en route from Frankfurt. They'll land at Westchester County Airport in about two hours. That doesn't give us much time ... please hold me."

She came into my arms and held me like it was forever. We left for the airport and she talked about her family on the way.

"I grew up on an Iowa farm with two older brothers and two sisters. We all learned to work and get along and now everyone is grown up and nobody wants to be a farmer any more. I guess it was just too much. Mom and Dad sent all of us kids to college and now we're too smart to spend our time with pigs and cows. It's not fair, but what can we do?" she said.

"You're doing it now. You're going home when you're needed. Anything I can do for you?" I said.

"You're doing it ... really, Bill ... I wish you could go along but just knowing you are here for me means everything. I'll call you when I get there," she said.

I walked her out to the corporate jet, a Falcon 50 painted yellow with a red stripe down the fuselage and a sunburst on the tail. The crew met us at the ramp. The uniformed pilot with a cocked hat and four hash marks on his sleeves began fawning all over Connie like she was the queen of the East. Come to think of it, she probably was to him. Sometimes I had problems remembering that she was one of the top five executives in a very large multi-national corporation.

"Good morning, Miss Wilson. Welcome aboard. We were over Yarmouth en route for Montreal, (he pronounced it the French way, Mor'eal), when we got the call to divert here to pick you up. Mr. Kamindorf is on board with Mr. Walinsky. You may know them. They're from our European division headed for the Chicago stockholder's meeting. Sorry to hear about your father. We'll be off as soon as we're refueled ..." He went on and on and he was really smooth. Connie turned to me at the bottom of the steps and put her arms around me.

"Thanks for the memories, Tiger. Save yourself for me. I'll be back." She gave me a kiss that nearly turned my brain to jelly, climbed the steps, and disappeared into the aircraft.

I watched her go and felt a stab of panic. She was leaving me and this was different. I was the one who usually did the leaving. I turned to find the pilot looking at me with a critical eye. "Will you be going with us, sir?" he said over the whine of the generator. He had suddenly become more professional.

"No, it's my turn to stay behind." I turned and looked at the refueling truck. "Are you running low on fuel? It's not that far to Chicago."

"After dropping our passengers off in Chicago, we have to make pickups in Seattle, Los Angeles, Phoenix and Dallas. If all goes well, we'll be back to Chicago by dinner time. This bird has long range capability, so by refueling here we'll save time." He was all business now, and I could see that he was a seasoned pilot. "Do you fly?" he asked.

"Yes, I used to. Not like this." I pointed to the aircraft. "I worked for State Mutual and I've been around the globe a few times. It must be a blast to fly this baby," I said.

"It is. Do you miss it?" he said, looking at me intently.

"I miss the flying. I don't miss the rest," I said.

"I can see that." He stuck out his hand and I took it.

"Have a safe journey," I said.

"You too, my friend," he said as he turned and started up the stairs.

The last I saw of Connie was her face in a window waving good bye as the sound of the turbines spooling up drowned out my thoughts.

I watched the airplane take off and stood there until the blinking light of its rotating beacon disappeared into the night sky. There was no other word for it: I was truly alone. Connie had come into my life at a time when I thought I needed no one. She was with me when bullets were flying past our heads. She had been kidnapped and both her personal and professional lives had nearly been destroyed because of people who were involved in cases I was investigating, but she always stuck by me. She was one hell of a woman and now she was gone and I was feeling helpless and lost, not a good thing for a macho insurance investigator like myself. I had to get a grip on it: get busy, get moving, do something. So I did. I started walking. It was still dark but dawn was not far away.

Airplanes had always fascinated me. When I worked

for State Mutual in New York City I traveled extensively in their corporate aircraft and many times I got a chance to sit up front. The pilots came to know me and were glad to sit back while I did some of the work. I even logged some time in the company's Aero Commander and King Air, both of which had been based at Westchester County Airport. I took flying lessons and earned my pilot's license there.

I decided to take a look around and see if maybe some of the old gang was still around. It was like coming home. I turned and started across the tarmac toward the corporate hangers. I should have known better. The security at airports has increased dramatically and I wasn't paying attention. I'd gone about a hundred yards and was coming around the tail of a Lear 24 when a voice in the darkness behind me brought me to a halt.

"Don't move, mister, or I'll blow your head off."

A short man dressed in overalls, holding a double-barreled shotgun, stepped out of the darkness ahead of me. "Put your hands up, buddy, and don't try anything stupid," he said.

I wasn't stupid, so just to prove it, I did as he said.

Chapter Three

THERE were two of them, and the little fellow in front held his twelve-gauge shotgun pointed at me about belly button high. I could tell it was a 12-gauge because it was right in front of me. He wore a baseball cap and I couldn't see much of his face because of the dark shadows, but he seemed very nervous. The hangar lights shone down onto the concrete apron behind him, reflecting on the parked airplanes and forming halos in the morning mist.

"Take it easy, guys. I'm no threat to you or anyone else ..."

"Shut up and stand still," the voice behind me said, and I realized it was a woman speaking or maybe a kid. I stood very still. "Check him over, Mickey, and be careful. He moves like a cat."

"That's me, fellows. I'm just a harmless kitten," I said, still thinking it was a joke.

"This isn't funny, mister," said the voice from behind. "These are real guns and you are in real trouble. It was a woman's voice for sure and Mickey looked familiar.

He moved behind me and I thought he might have to put down the shotgun to do a thorough body search. I didn't have to worry, however, because he held the muzzle of the gun in the small of my back and used his other hand to pat me down. The Glock 17 was in the trunk of my Caddy. I hadn't thought that I would need a firearm while walking around an airport. My Special Forces knife was back at the cottage on the North Fork of Long Island where I should have been right at that moment. Then my memory cells kicked in.

'You haven't grown any taller since the last time I saw you, Mickey, but you sure look a lot older," I said. His hand stopped its search.

'Do I know you, mister?" He said, stepping back. I turned very slowly.

"William Thackery O'Keefe?" said the voice as she stepped out into the soft reflection of the hangar lights.

"Billy Jean Furman, as I live and breathe! How are you doing, Babe?" I said.

She looked better than ever: the dark round eyes, short brown hair, and a figure that could still win a beauty contest even now after four children and twenty-five years or more of marriage.

"What the hell are you doing here? Are you working for them?" she said, as if she were spitting sour grape seeds.

"There must be some sort of mistake, Billy Jean. I'm not working for anyone. I just said goodbye to a friend on that Falcon 50 and decided to wander over here to see if any of the old gang was still around. I'm sorry if I scared you," I said.

"You're not what scares me, O'Keefe." She kept searching the area as if expecting an attack at any moment. "Are you alone?"

"Yes," I said. "I was just wandering around. Look,

what's going on here? Why all the hardware and sneaking around?" I asked.

"We can't talk here," she said. "Let's go inside." She pointed toward the large hangar behind us. "Mickey! Stay alert. You know what to do if there's any trouble. O'Keefe, you stay ahead of me." She held her gun up and kept looking around as we walked.

I walked slowly but kept a wary eye out for any movement around us. I didn't want to become involved in any accidental shootings. Billy Jean stayed just behind me and to my right. I hadn't seen her in almost seven years, but she looked as good as ever and she still had her Italian spirit. She was always a gutsy little babe. Her husband, Anthony, flew for State Mutual and was one of the guys who let me sit up front and fly the company airplane.

Billy Jean was a fully qualified commercial pilot and flight instructor with ratings in multi-engine recip and turbine-equipped aircraft. It was rumored she could fly circles around Tony, but that was never confirmed because she always deferred to him. "He's the chief pilot in the family," she would say. "I'm just his co-pilot," and that's the way it was. We went through an access door in the larger door of the hangar and she locked it behind her.

"You know where the office is. We'll talk in there," she said.

The hangar was jammed with airplanes and I recognized two King Airs and an Aero Commander 690 as well as some smaller twin engine aircraft and single engine Cessnas. We entered the office in the back right corner of the hangar and Billy Jean pointed with her Smith and Wesson .38 to a chair at the side of her desk.

"I'm still not sure why you're here, O'Keefe. Part of me wants to shoot you and another part of me wants to kiss you. It's up to you so convince me which it will be," she said.

'I always get excited when you talk tough to me, lady," I joked, but she just raised the gun and pointed it at my head. "Okay ... okay, obviously something very serious is happening here and I am not in on it, so I'll repeat what I said before."

I told her about Connie Wilson, Willie Monk, and the cases I had worked the last few years. I tried to convince her I was not connected in any way with State Mutual or its president, John Stanley, but she still seemed skeptical.

"Do you remember a place called East Harbour out on Long Island where there was an insurance scam and a series of murders for profit two years ago?" I asked.

"Vaguely, Bill. I don't keep up on all the local gossip," she said.

"How about SARTXE, the Senator Cantrelli-Jersey Mutual scandal last year? Surely you didn't miss that one. One of your colleagues, Kenny Warren's brother, Ted Warren, a helicopter pilot, was murdered by Cuban mercenaries."

"Oh God! Were you involved in that, O'Keefe? Why, that was unbelievable! Didn't it involve the President of the United States and some large insurance companies, as well as the Navy and the United Nations?" she said.

"Ahh ... you can read after all," I said, relaxing.

"Oh yes, now I remember something about your children being kidnapped and some sort of illegal paramilitary operation. Holy smoke, O'Keefe, you are some sort of heavy-duty dude. That was really big time and as I think of it now there was a very high body count," she said.

"I'm a modest, unassuming insurance investigator who just said goodbye to his one and only love and now I'm at loose ends, alone, left with nothing to do," I said.

"Yeah, sure," she said. "You must make tons of money."

"Not always. I work for ten percent of what I save or recover for the client. If I don't deliver, I don't get paid," I said.

"Sounds like a real nice life. No attachments, no overhead, no mortgage, no boss, no worry, no fuss. Wish I had the same deal."

"So what is your deal, Billy Jean? Why all the security? Where's all this paranoia coming from?" I said.

"It's not paranoia. Someone is trying to take it all away from us. Tony has disappeared and the sheriff is at the door. We have the aircraft in the hangar and a twenty-four hour armed patrol outside. It's horrible! I don't know what to do." She broke down crying.

My first impulse was to throw my arms around the little lady and give her some comfort, but I knew this woman better. She was a tough little trooper and huggy-kissy was not her style, so I waited and looked around the office while she worked it out. Pictures covered the walls, each picture showing the growth of the family: Anthony, Billy Jean, and their four children. A later picture of the oldest, Tony Jr., showed him in an Air Force flight suit, standing next to an F-15 Eagle.

He was the spitting image of his father, who had served in Vietnam. Pictures of military and civilian airplanes were mixed in and there was one of Tony with his C-130 and crew when he was in the Air Force. Flight certificates, merit awards, and certifications ran along the top row, and to finish the gallery there was a cut-off shirttail framed on a plaque with Billy Jean's name and the date of her first solo.

"I'm sorry, Bill," she apologized, red eyed, blowing her nose on a tissue. "I usually hold it together but it's really tough being alone."

"Where's Tony?" I asked.

"I wish I knew. He went out last night to get a newspaper and never came back. He's never done that before. I called the police, the hospitals, everyone, but there isn't a trace of him and nobody has seen him. His car was parked in the driveway this morning with a note on the front seat saying that he will be away for a few days and that's it. The note wasn't even in his handwriting," she said.

"Who's behind this?" I asked. "Do you owe anyone money? Any gambling, drinking, or wild women?" I said, winking to let her know I was kidding around, only I wasn't.

"That's just it, I don't know. It's all so crazy. You know me, O'Keefe. I'm not an airhead and I'm certainly not a Weeping Willy, but this thing is really scary and I don't know what to do about it. She started to cry again. I could see that this was going to take time. That was okay with me; I had nothing but time now that Connie was gone and I could use something to keep busy and out of trouble. Little did I know how much trouble I was getting into.

Chapter Four

I walked to a table where there was a two-burner hot plate with a small saucepan on it filled with water: airport coffee machine. To top it off, I found instant coffee with modified imitation re-constituted cream substitute and white sugar on the shelf below. At least the sugar looked real and there was nothing crawling around in it.

"Why don't you begin at the beginning and I'll make us a pot of this delicious airport office coffee on this here space age coffee maker while you talk," I said, turning the hot plate on.

Billy Jean talked as I stirred. The natural beauty of her Mediterranean features gave way to the stress and the long hours she had endured, and she appeared pale and shaken as she related the story. Things were going well, the bills were paid, the contracts were steady, and life was looking pretty good. The kids were grown and only one still lived at home. That was Mickey, the little fellow outside in the overalls. Linda and Jimmy Linn, the next oldest, were working into the business as fully qualified pilots carrying most of the workload and Tony Jr. would join them after his tour in the Air Force. Everything was going well.

Suddenly one day two very hard looking types in blue

suits came and told Tony to get out. They handed him eviction papers and a notice of foreclosure. Tony told them to get lost and they roughed him up and trashed the office. A sheriff's deputy showed up a week later with an Execution and Notice of Seizure. Billy Jean reached in the desk drawer and handed me some papers.

"Who were the two goons?" I asked, setting up two cups.

"We have no idea. The foreclosure notice isn't even from our bank. We called and asked what was going on and the bank president said our loan had been discounted, whatever the heck that means. Then Tony disappeared, and yesterday morning we caught someone trying to steal one of the King Airs," she said.

"Who was it? Did you get his name?" I asked, pouring hot water into the two cups.

"I don't know. We turned him over to the police. They let him go and we never saw him again. The police said he was a repossessor and that he had papers for the airplane. I can't believe they bought that story and let him go. Those airplanes are all paid for. The mortgage is for the buildings and equipment. We have separate loans for everything else. Then I got this telephone call last night and a really strange voice with an accent told me to sign some papers they were sending over and then leave the premises or I would be very sorry. That's why we were outside tonight. We were trying to catch whoever delivered the papers but instead you showed up," she said.

"Here," I said, handing her a cup of coffee, "drink this and take it easy. First of all these papers are bogus.

They're copies of copies. Even the cutting and pasting job on the original was sloppy. You can see the paste lines. Notices of foreclosure and seizure must be served by an officer of the court, a deputy or constable, who must identify himself in person. The paperwork must be original and have the seal of the authorizing body, the court in this case, stamped in an appropriate and visible place on the documents," I said, pointing to the bottom of the page.

"Someone is trying to pull a fast one," I said, continuing. "This has all the earmarks of small time mob activities. Nobody in their right mind resorts to extortion and intimidation like this any more. Has anyone shown an interest lately in your hangar facilities here on the field? I know this is really prime real estate and there are people who want to move onto the flight line. Airlines will pay big money for this kind of space."

"Somebody from the Dominican Republic came by last year, but we turned them down and they never came back. Nobody has shown an interest since then," she said, sipping her coffee.

"Do you have their names?" I asked.

"I don't think so. We didn't pay any attention to them," she said.

"See what you can find. I'll need your mortgage papers, lease agreements, incorporation papers, a list of your employees and their personnel records, and ..."

"Wait, just hold it. I appreciate your interest but frankly I don't think we can afford you. The way things are ten percent of nothing is equal to nothing. They have us over a barrel. We're due for our yearly FAA operator's inspection and flight check next week, and if I can't produce a healthy chief pilot, they'll pull our Air Taxi Certificate and that means we lose our business. The FAA will shut us down and we'll be out in the cold. The voice on the phone mentioned that. It's all academic without Tony and the certificate to operate," she said.

"You don't have to worry about paying me. You and Tony always treated me like a friend. Even when I left State Mutual and went on my own with Willie Monk, you were there when I needed a quick trip and couldn't pay up front. When I took flying lessons you carried me on the books for over a year while I paid my bill. I can't guarantee I will find Tony in time for the flight check. I have some ideas that may help, however, so if you're willing, I'm at your disposal."

"Billy Jean stood up, walked over to where I was standing by the windows and said, "I guess I have decided to give you that kiss after all," and she did.

We talked for a while and I looked over the company's papers. There was nothing remarkable about them. The first mortgage on the business, held by the Bryn Mawr Bank and Trust, was secured by the hangar and the equipment in it. The total came to thirteen million, two hundred thousand dollars. The payments were up to date. The business had fared well, even in a shrinking economy, and Tony had managed to pick up extra income by running mail and freight contracts with several of the overnight parcel delivery companies. He had gone head to head with the airlines in some cases and beaten them out ... very impressive, indeed. So, who wanted him out of the way? Were the airlines miffed at

Tony and Billy Jean? If so, why didn't they just buy them out? Did someone want their hangar? Not recently. Was Tony into something shady or downright illegal?

"No! Definitely not!" said Billy Jean.

"How about gambling?" I asked.

"Never! Tony would never gamble. You know him, Bill. How could you even think such a thing?" she asked, looking hurt.

"I am sorry but I have to approach this objectively. No one goes to this much trouble to scare somebody out of business without good reason. Help me think. Why would anyone do this?" I asked.

"I've racked my brain, and I can't come up with any reason. I have a business to run and it's on the brink of going down the drain. I'm a chief pilot short, the wolves are at the door, and all I know is I have to put up four airplanes today and I don't have enough pilots to do it. I have a trip to Montreal at noon, another to Cincinnati, one to Dallas and Houston with a return tomorrow morning, and a trip to Miami, not to mention two ground schools and twenty-five student pilots looking for flight time. I don't have the time or energy to stay up all night pacing the fortress walls to fend off an attack from an unknown enemy," she said.

"What you are saying then is you need protection," I said. It was growing light outside and I was feeling the need to get moving.

"Yes, I need protection and peace of mind. I can't concentrate with all this craziness going on," she said.

"I can give you protection. Peace of mind is up to you. There are some things we have to do, however, before all hell breaks loose and it will as soon as I start probing around. We'll need a couple of days to set up and get ready," I said.

"This may sound crazy, but I don't think we have a couple of days," said Billy Jean. "The loan payment is due tomorrow, that's Friday, and I don't have the money. No one will talk to us about refinancing. It's like we're lepers. Everything's on a cash only basis. No one will cash our checks and we can't deposit any of the money we have coming in. I tried to open another account and the bank refused. They said there was a lock on all our assets."

"That's the first thing we'll do then. You need cash, so we'll go to the people that have it to give," I said.

"You are kidding, aren't you? Where can you lay your hands on that sort of money, or shouldn't I ask?" she said.

"We have our ways my dear." I did my Dracula act and Billy Jean laughed. She looked better laughing and I felt better too. Cry a little, lie a little, joke a little. Makes everyone feel better. Billy Jean raised a good question, however. Where, indeed, would I be able to put my hands on big money? Granted I had contacts, and to some of them 13.2 million was petty cash, but would they spring for it on such short notice? The other question was, who were we dealing with and would it do any good to make the mortgage payment?

"I have an idea," said Billy Jean. "What if we didn't make the mortgage payment? That would make them come after us, and then we could find out who they are."

"So far you've been lucky because all the paperwork and so-called court documents are fakes. Granted they managed to shut down your financial dealings and that's serious but until now you haven't missed a loan payment or broken any laws. If you can't make the payment tomorrow and you don't produce a chief pilot by next Wednesday for the FAA inspectors, then you're out of business. So, let's concentrate on the loan payment. I'll find a way to flush out the bad guys. Believe me, once they know I'm here they'll show up and you may see some things you'll wish you hadn't," I said.

"You're right. I'll have to learn to trust your judgment. It's all beyond me," she said. "I'm not used to giving up control over things like this. Are you really sure you can help me? Be honest, Bill."

"Sometimes we have to learn to trust the people around us. More important, we have to learn to trust ourselves. You taught me that when I took flying lessons, remember? I asked you one day how a flight instructor knows when to take the controls away from a student. You said it was a matter of experience, but more than that it depends on how much a flight instructor trusts his own ability to get out of a potentially disastrous situation," I said.

"That's right. Most people think the flight instructor makes decisions based on how much he trusts the student but that isn't it at all. So, what is your point, O'Keefe?" she said.

"I'm not a flight instructor. I have a lot of experience being in tight situations in the corporate world. I have confidence in my own abilities to take control and save your business. I've been there before and I know what to do and I don't scare that easy," I said.

"That's for sure. You didn't even blink when Mickey pointed that shotgun at you. You just took control of the situation," she said.

"That's right, and if I had been a real bad guy, both you and Mickey would probably be dead right now. You're rank amateurs."

"I resent that," she said, flaring. "I am an expert shot with that gun. I hit whatever I aim at and Mickey is an expert skeet shooter."

"Yes, but have you ever killed anyone or been under fire?" I said.

"Well, no, but ..." she said, hesitating.

"No buts about it. I don't doubt your courage, Billy Jean, but if we have to go up against any hard cases you should let me handle them. I think we're dealing with professional criminals and they don't play by the same rules as decent folks. So, from now on, let's suspend the rule book," I said.

"But what rules are we playing by?" she asked.

"I'll teach you. Follow me through, as the flight instructor says."

"What do you want me to do?" she asked.

"First of all, cancel all your student appointments and the ground school. Tell them you're taking a vacation. We don't want innocent civilians around with the bad guys trying to strong arm us. Stand guard and watch for intruders. Today's criminals use automatic weapons and they don't care who gets hurt. We need more than a pistol and a shotgun. If Tony has been abducted, we're dealing with more than you can handle on your own," I said.

"Shouldn't we call the FBI or somebody like that?" she asked. "I'd never forgive myself if something happens to Tony. I could never go on without him," she said, beginning to tear up again.

"The FBI might scare them away and then we'd have a real problem finding Tony. We don't want to take any chances. As long as they think they can scare you into leaving, they'll keep Tony alive," I said, as the phone on Billy Jean's desk rang and she answered it.

"Furman Airways ... Yes ... Yes ... When? Roger that ...Okay." She replaced the receiver and looked at me.

"One of our aircraft, Nine One Charlie, is an emergency inbound on one engine!" she said, standing up.

Chapter Five

BILLY Jean took a black handheld radio with a small whip antenna and a pair of binoculars from her desk drawer. She was all business now as she headed out the door and I followed her.

"That's our Miami run, King Air N6891C. Left yesterday morning with a load of mail and returned through Boston. The plane's empty, but he's a green kid." We were walking quickly through the hangar. "Damn, that's Jimmy Linn. He's only twenty-three and has less than five hundred hours multi-time," she said.

We met Mickey at the door of the hangar, still carrying the shotgun. He was out of breath. "Mom, Jimmy Linn..."

"I know, Mickey. The tower just called me. He declared an emergency over Hartford, says his left engine exploded and caught fire. He's got it under control ... he'll call soon ..." We came to the edge of the apron where the taxiway began and we had a good view of the active north-south runway.

"Furman, this is ninety-one Charlie on company ..." The radio crackled to life.

"Roger, Jimmy Linn, this is Furman, how's it going?" Billy Jean answered, her voice calm and cool.

"I'm okay, Mom. Left engine blew up ... but fire is out ...over."

"Good work Jimmy Linn ... remember now ... keep it hot over the fence ... it'll settle fast on you." The strain showed on her face.

"Got it, Mom ... not to worry. Had a good trip ... I'm buying breakfast."

"You're on, Jimmy ... we'll be waiting." She was a very cool lady. "That's my next to oldest. He's just like his father. My oldest, Tony Junior, is in the Air Force ... F-15 pilot. Come to think of it, he's just like his father, too," she said, with a slight smile.

"Or his mother," I offered.

"Yeah, well ... we don't talk about that. Tony's the chief pilot of this family," she said.

The radio crackled again. Ninety-one Charlie was ten miles out. The tower read him the numbers: wind direction and speed, altimeter, runway in use, report entering down wind, emergency equipment standing by, good luck! The controller sounded bored and uninvolved but I knew better. I'd been in the tower and I knew the stress they were under. Pilots died in a blaze of glory. Air traffic controllers died a little each day. Every head in that tower would be turned to watch this landing. Every controller in the New York Common I room (New York Approach Control) would be aware that ninety-one Charlie lost an engine. The Logan controllers in Boston and the Center controllers in Nashua would be quiet and more attentive until they got the word that ninety-one Charlie was down safely.

Jimmy Linn reported a long downwind and a wide

base leg, making shallow right turns into his good engine. We could see him as he set up his approach from the south, a long shallow final.

Billy Jean raised her binoculars and followed his progress. "He's not trailing any smoke. Gear's coming down, looks okay. There's the flaps ... atta boy ... keep it hot, son ..." Billy Jean said, clucking like a mother hen, or more like a good flight instructor as if she were sitting right next to her son. "Keep it hot ... that's it ... power back ... no torque now, straighten it out and flare ... nice ... very nice. Good flying just like his father ... real cool," she said with pride in her voice.

"What'd he do wrong, Mickey?" she said turning.

"Left his flaps down too long after touch down," said Mickey.

"Right! Gotta get those flaps off so the airplane stays down ... no skidding or skipping around," she said, always the flight instructor.

We waited as he taxied into the tie-down area with the fire trucks and ambulance trailing close behind.

"There'll be hell to pay for this," said Billy Jean. "We can't afford an engine change right now."

"How long will it take?" I asked.

"Depends on the damage: a day, a month or maybe never. It all depends on what we find. Mickey, as soon as the fire guys get out of the way, get the aircraft inside and start pulling that engine. I'll call Engine Reworks in Wichita as soon as you tell me what we've got."

"Right, Mom, but I'll need help," he said, turning away.

"I'll call in two extras from over at Delta. You just get started, okay?"

Mickey gave the thumbs up and we started toward the crippled airplane. Firemen were crawling all over the left wing, looking inside the engine cowling, inspecting the landing gear and wing. The door opened and a young man, looking much like his father, descended the stairs.

"Not bad for an amateur, right, Mom?" He gave me a quick glance and a once over.

"Not bad at all, Jimmy Linn. What the hell happened?" She walked up to him and gave him a hug, then led him off to one side.

"Well, I departed Boston-Logan on runway four-right. Of course I was IFR. They wouldn't let me slip out any other way. I was cleared to 12,000 feet but they stopped me at 6,500 for inbound traffic from the north, so I waited until I was over Millis and cancelled my IFR flight plan. It was overcast, bottoms of the clouds at 8000 feet so I stayed around 6,500 until Hartford where it started to break up." He spoke as if in a trance, like he was flying the airplane all over again. "I decided to go on top. When I passed through 10,200, it happened. It felt like a thump and sounded like a firecracker in a soup can."

"You must have been pretty scared," said Mickey.

"I've never felt so alone," said Jimmy Linn. "While I was shutting down the engine, I went through some clouds. When I broke out, I was almost vertical. Not good ... not good at all," he said.

"So, the thing blew at around 10,200?" Billy Jean repeated, prompting him.

"Yes, and there was fire and smoke right away. I cut the fuel, feathered the prop, punched the fire extinguisher, and prayed. I came out of it at 6,000, trimmed it up and called ATC."

"You did good," said Billy Jean, patting him on the shoulder. She put her head close to his and said, "Let's talk about this in private," and she led him away toward the hangar. I hung around the airplane and listened to the comments of the fire crew.

"Kid handled it like a pro ... made it look easy," said one man.

"Probably was easy. The hard part must have been when this thing blew up. Look at the mess in there," said another.

"Hear they're having troubles. This is what happens when an outfit goes cheap on maintenance." One of the firemen saw me and silenced the others.

"Can we help you, buddy? This is a restricted area ya know!" The speaker was a big man with 'Chief' printed on his helmet.

"Insurance investigator," I said, flashing my I.D. "I was doing an inspection when this happened."

"Kinda early to be inspectin', isn't it?" he said.

"Best time ... nobody in the way. Looks like I hit the jackpot." I pointed to the damaged engine. "What do you see up there?"

"Real mess," said one of the firemen. "Turbine blades all busted up, holes in everything and some fire damage. You'd expect more fire with an explosion like this. It's just like somebody stuck a monkey wrench in the air intake and it got sucked all the way through."

"I'll hang around while they take it apart. Take some pictures. We've had problems with these rebuilds and the insuring companies want to know why. This is the third one this year and all from the same place, Engine Reworks in Wichita." I said.

"No kidding," the Chief said, impressed. "You mean this is what you do? Go around checking out broken airplanes?"

"Among other things. We're interested in safety and let's face it, nobody needs higher insurance rates. If some rebuild shop is using parts that are not certified American or skimping on repairs, we want to know it. Hell, just last month we found automotive spark plugs in an aircraft right from the factory. I can't mention any names, of course. The pilot had to land in a cornfield because the spark plugs fouled and he lost power. It was nighttime. Did a hell of a job getting it down. You can't imagine the pile of insurance claims and lawsuits that created."

"You think these guys are skimping on maintenance?" the Chief asked, indicating the Furman Airways hangar.

"I doubt it. Furman has always had a good reputation. We'll check everything but I can't see Tony and Billy Jean sending their own son up in an aircraft that wasn't all right," I said.

"You got a point there, but rumor has it they're in trouble and to watch them to make sure they don't do anything stupid. We've got a good safety record here and we intend to keep it that way," he said.

"I can believe it. I was impressed at how you got into action and stuck with the aircraft. You and your team are to be commended. I wish some of the bigger airports were as good," I said.

"Hey, thanks. We really appreciate your saying that. We don't get much credit for what we do around here," he said, shaking my hand, and I left them to their work.

It was sun-up and the sky was a pale clear blue. The north wind had passed through the area taking the rain, sleet, and fog with it, and a warmer southwesterly was moving in, promising a brighter, more comfortable day. A B-737 Trans Con was moving away from the main terminal for its morning hop to somewhere, and a small commuter twin engine aircraft was landing on the active runway.

There's something about an airport that stirs the blood and brings the spirit of adventure to the surface of one's being. The flying bug bit me when I was working in New York City. I was living in Scarsdale with my wife and three children: Timothy, Samantha, and Jonathan. I couldn't stand the quiet life of an insurance executive on the nine-to-five treadmill so I went looking for excitement and ended up at the airport taking flying lessons. Nothing had changed and I still love to fly.

I watched the B-737 take off and walked back to the hangar where Mickey and a line-boy were pulling the King Air inside. Billy Jean and Jimmy Linn were in the office and I joined them. She introduced me. Billy Jean was born and raised in Fort Worth, Texas and met Tony at Carswell Air Force Base. After Vietnam, they moved back to his hometown, White Plains, and started the business.

"We'll have to wait until Mickey pulls that engine before we know anything more," she said. "Jimmy Linn says there were no indications of any problems before the explosion. That engine only had three hundred hours on it since major overhaul. I'll bet someone tampered with it while Jimmy Linn was on the ground in Boston," she said, glancing his way.

"Oh, Mother! That's ridiculous. Who would do such a thing? I told you, I just left the airplane for a few minutes. I had to take a leak. How could anyone do something to an engine in such a short time? It was right out in the open where every one could see it," he said.

"Why don't we just wait and see," I said. "It's easy to become paranoid with things the way they are right now. By the way, have you explained everything to Jimmy Linn?"

There was a look of resignation on her face. "I thought it would be better to wait and see what develops," she said.

"It might be better to clue him in now so he'll understand why I'm here and why you're standing guard day and night," I said.

She told Jimmy Linn what was happening and he was genuinely shocked. Billy Jean looked tired and I thought that she was probably losing her ability to reason. As I thought about it, I realized I'd lost a few hours of sleep too and I was hungry. I said as much and Jimmy Linn volunteered to go out to get some eats.

"If it wasn't for these boys, I'd be dead right now," said Billy Jean after he left.

"You have a daughter, too. Where is she?" I asked.

"Linda? She's due in before noon from the Dallas-Houston run. She stops at Newark and off-loads, then hops up here. She's my pet, only twenty two-years old. I don't tell her this, but she's a better pilot than I am," said Billy Jean.

"So, all your children fly except Mickey?" I asked.

"He flies too. He has his commercial license and multi-rating but Mickey likes engines. Give him something mechanical and he loses himself in it. I'm glad, because we need someone around here to keep an eye on things while the rest of us are off in the wild blue yonder."

"You have quite an operation with these mail and freight contracts," I said. "Do the airlines object to the competition?"

"Actually, it's the airlines that put us into the business. The industry trend is toward bigger aircraft and fewer flights. Some of their flights are virtual cattle cars with what they call high-density configuration seating," Billy Jean said.

"The loading and unloading of these big aircraft takes more time, especially since the airlines have cut ground personnel and backup equipment in order to reduce costs. It's a free-for-all up there in the skies as well as at the airports. The big airlines have discontinued services to many smaller airports, so that leaves an opening for small air taxi operators like us. We get to fill in the cracks in the system. We also catch the overflow.

The airlines are always calling us to fly the freight and passengers they can't handle," she continued, warming to her subject.

"The biggest problem in this business is capital, money for airplanes and operations. We've solved that problem by operating used equipment and keeping it within the family. Tony and I did most of the flying before. Now the kids are taking over. We pay them half what they'd be paid elsewhere but they get a piece of the company, which was worth a lot up until now. They understand that and accept it. At least they did. Now I don't know what will happen. You know, Bill, it really hasn't hit me yet that Tony's gone. I just won't accept it! I know he's all right and I expect him to walk through that door at any moment. I can't take much more of this and if he doesn't come back ... I don't know what I'll do." She began to get teary-eyed again.

"Hang in there, Billy Jean. He'll be back and things will be okay. I guarantee it," I said.

I gave her a hug, which turned into a kiss and I felt a little guilty. Husband out of town, bad guys threatening to take over, poor little lady needs comforting and protection and whadaya know? Along comes O'Keefe, good guy, riding a white stallion and wearing a white hat. Connie is out of town so who's to know? However, Willie Monk had something to say about this sort of situation.

He used to say, "O'Keefe, before you diddle around with some good lookin' chick while you're workin' a case, just tally up the pot and see where the money's hid. While you're diddlin' around, the bad guys may be gettin' away with the whole pot of gold." Then he would say, "Pay attention, damn it! Pay attention to what's important," and poke, poke with his fingers and that damned stogie.

"Are you all right, Bill?" Billy Jean asked, her cheeks flushed.

"Yes, sure, I was just ... uhh, day dreaming." I let go of her. "Listen, my car is in the hourly pay parking lot. I think I'll move it over to this side. Will you be all right while I'm gone?" I said.

"Sure," she said. She turned to look in a mirror on the wall, a weak smile on her face as she straightened her hair. "Don't worry, I won't hold you to that kiss. Call it harmless, all right?" She smiled for real, a smile that said everything really was all right.

"That's just it, Billy Jean, it wasn't harmless. You and I both know it." I turned and walked out of the office before I made a complete fool of myself.

I went back through the main terminal and out into the parking lot and no one seemed to notice. Willie Monk was right, I needed to pay attention. Billy Jean was a strikingly beautiful woman who could turn any man's head. It was seven years since I'd last seen her and she was more beautiful than ever, or was I just a lonely old fool? She married Tony when she was young and the four children came one right after the other. It was hard work and she told me that there were times when Tony was flying C-130's that she didn't think she would make it as a young mother.

Billy Jean and I had shared our moments, here and there. You know what I mean, a moment of realization that we liked each other, that we were attracted to each other: a touch, a brushing of the hand, a playful punch, the meeting of the eyes, but she was a married woman then, and I was a married man. So what was so different now? Nothing and everything. We were still both committed to someone else but the difference now was that we were both alone. Willie Monk's words hammered at my brain.

"Pay attention, O'Keefe!" he would say: poke, poke with that stogie.

Chapter Six

I took a small sail bag with some of my 'tools', out of the trunk and got in the front seat of the Caddy. I strapped the Glock 17 in its holster onto my left ankle with two spare clips. This added extra weight but it was better than having someone spot a concealed weapon under my sports jacket. I was licensed to carry a weapon but people become very upset if they discover you're wearing a hidden gun. It may not be a problem in Texas or Arizona, but around the New York City area there are only two reasons why a person wears a concealed weapon: either you're a police officer or a criminal. Many law-abiding citizens have permits but the general public tends to think in black and white and the media is constantly banging away at gun control, creating a culture of fear.

The Glock holds seventeen nine-millimeter cartridges. You can carry one in the chamber as well. I don't do that. Seventeen shots is a lot and two extra clips bring the number to fifty-one. Most firefights are settled long before that. The gun is lightweight with a double action trigger for that first shot. Just pull the trigger and bang.

These were dangerous people that Tony and Billy Jean were up against. The prize was Furman Airways, mortgaged for $13.2 million, yet its net worth was more like $50 million. Used aircraft and prime hangar space were worth big bucks and someone was playing rough and dirty to get it. They had a big surprise coming because they didn't know about me.

I paid the parking attendant and followed the airport access road out to the main highway, turned left as if I were headed home and drove at thirty mph. Two cars were following me and I kept a wary eye on them both. The Furman Airways phones might be bugged so I decided that now was a good time to make some calls.

I moved into the right lane and slowed down. One of the cars passed me, the driver giving me the finger as he floored it, roaring down the highway. The other car, a full-sized dark brown Ford sedan with no special markings, slowed down and pulled in behind me. It was no ordinary car. It had tinted glass so I could not see who was driving but one thing got my attention. Its chassis was jacked up and the engine sounded big. Even with my windows closed I could hear it. That car had speed built into it, more than my Caddy would ever have.

I drove at a modest speed and the Ford stayed behind me. In New York if a fellow is driving too slow you pass him. For the average New Yorker life is a serious race and you never let up or someone will pass you or run over you. I picked up my car phone and dialed a private number. It was early but I knew it would be answered.

"Deputy Woo here."

"Woo, this is O'Keefe. Where are you?"

"I'm on Post Road, headed for court. What's up?"

"I have a tail and I don't know who it is. I'm just

a few miles south of the airport on Rt. 684, headed southbound."

"I'll wait for you at the Hutchinson River Parkway. Go east on Rt. 287 toward Rye. There's a good spot for a take down there. What am I looking for?"

"It's an older dark brown Ford sedan, tinted windows, very plain but lots of soup so be careful. I'm turning onto the Hutchinson River Parkway now. I'm just a quarter mile from Rt. 287," I said.

"I'm there now. I see your Caddy and your tail. Keep it coming. By the way, what am I getting into?" he asked.

"Extortion, possible kidnapping and maybe attempted murder."

"Why is it, O'Keefe, that every time I hear your voice I expect World War Three to break out?" he said.

"You're just paranoid ... but stay alert," I said.

I saw Woo's unmarked green sedan pull out behind the Ford, which was about a hundred yards behind me as I continued east on Rt. 287 toward Rye.

"All right, about a half mile ahead on the right is a pull off. It's a maintenance stop for state equipment. Pull off there and pretend to check your tires. We'll see what happens," said Woo.

I slowed down and pulled off at the spot he indicated. The Ford pulled to a stop about thirty yards behind me. I left my engine running, got out and walked to the front of the car, bent over as if to check the front tire, and reached down to my ankle for the Glock. A car door slammed and I looked up to see a short, dark-complected man coming toward me. Woo pulled over about ten feet behind the Ford and the dance was on.

The man walking toward my car looked back and saw Woo getting out, turned and ran for the Ford, opened the passenger door and jumped in just as it took off. Woo was already back in his car and the two of them raced off down the road, both powerful engines roaring at top speed. I jumped into my car and followed them, the engine in my Caddy missing as I accelerated.

Kim had the jump on the Ford and passed it in less than a quarter mile. Then he cut them off and deliberately spun his vehicle around in front, causing the driver of the Ford to spin his wheel and jam on his brakes. They came to a screaming halt side by each and the Ford made an attempt to pull away, heading back the way he came. I arrived just in time to pin him in between Woo's car and the center guardrail. We were out of our cars and had them covered before they could move.

"Nicely done," I said to Kim. "Where'd you learn that trick?"

"Just thought it up," he said, handcuffing the driver.

The shorter man in the passenger side tried to come at me, but I took him with a straight kick to the chest and he sat down hard on the centerline of the highway.

"You took your time. I could have been hurt, you know," I said, as I patted down the short one.

"Not a chance, you had them outnumbered," Kim said.

I asked them some questions but neither one would respond. They appeared to be South American but I couldn't tell.

"Now, who the hell are they and what am I supposed to do with them?" asked Woo as we put them in the back of his car. "Do you want them booked? And if so, what are the charges?"

"I need to know who they are, so can you hold them for a few hours, like until five o'clock when everything is closed? Get me pictures, fingerprints, anything that will help me connect them. Call me at this number. It's Furman Airways but be careful what you say. The phones may be bugged," I said.

"Okay, you got it. Just clue me in later about what's going on. I don't like working in the dark," he said, and he drove off.

I moved my car to the side of the road and did the same with the Ford. There was no registration, nothing to identify who they were. They were dark skinned with black hair but neither of them had spoken a word. I found a bottle of Thomas' Sapphire Bay Rum, un Producto de la Rupublica Dominicana in the glove compartment. I found a few chewing gum wrappers in the back seat and an old worn out windshield wiper. The car was an older model car and under the hood I found a very big engine with some modifications.

The numbers 457 were stamped on the valve covers. A big power plant, too big for city driving. I got a surprise in the trunk: several cardboard boxes were filled with a sort of bulb or root, covered with red dirt. I put one of the bulbs in my jacket pocket and closed the boxes. The shipping labels read SPD (Speedy Parcel Delivery): Fernandes Nurseries, Southold, N.Y.

Things were beginning to fit together. I now had two

faces to put to the events that Billy Jean Furman had described to me this morning. I closed the trunk, tossed the keys on the front seat, and departed the scene, as they say.

I thought about a previous case that Willie and I had several years before as I drove back to the airport. There had been a rash of robberies and fires on the south side of Chicago. The insurance companies did not like being ripped off. It gives them a bad name. Willie and I had a reputation for getting the job done without a lot of red tape, so we went to Chicago and started investigating.

We didn't get very far before it became obvious that nobody wanted to talk to us. "What we got here is a conspiracy to delude," said Willie. "These people all got the same story. So what that tells me, being a student of human nature that I am, it tells me that they all work for the same outfit."

That was clear as mud and I told Willie so but he just kept right on like I wasn't even there.

"Think about it. These robberies all involved breaking and entering. There was the usual damage, like broken doors and windows and blown safes and walls all broke up and all that was covered by insurance, right?" He pointed at me like I was the culprit.

"Right," I said, "and every claim was filed in an expeditious manner and the repairs were made and the claims paid, and the police never connected anyone to the robberies. Each robbery involved a large sum of cash. The owners had cash register tapes, bank drafts, tallies and account books to back up their claim. The insurance was paid up and the damage was limited to the break-in," I said.

"So, it's like I said. They's all workin' for the same guy," Willie said, pointing his finger at me again, and then he pulled the trigger, so-to-speak. "They's deluded if they think we're this dumb."

We checked the adjusters, contractors and relatives of everyone and came to Joe Merchant, owner of the Great Lakes Consolidated Builders. His uncle, Simon Krieger, a City Councilman and aging crony from the old Mayor Daley years, had a son who was a developer. He bought up all the properties that were hit by arson.

"Dumb, real dumb. Did they think that nobody'd figure it out? We're gonna bury these jerks," Willie said," as we rode the elevator up to the 65th floor of the Chicago Trade Tower to meet with the insurance company reps. "It don't pay to steal from insurance companies. They'll hunt ya down no matter how long it takes."

The Attorney General, who was running for re-election, jumped on it like a bulldog on a raw hamburger and we went home with a check for our retainer and expenses. Three years later, we received a very generous check for our ten percent after all the bad guys had been convicted and the properties had been confiscated and resold. "See what I mean?" said Willie. "It don't pay to mess with the pros."

Chapter Seven

EXTORTION and intimidation were not new in the insurance business but, Billy Jean Furman was up against hard core criminals. The trip back to the airport was uneventful and my arrival at Furman Airways was a timely one. Two more King Airs were on the apron in front of the hangar and Mickey had the damaged engine fully exposed. Several men stood around peering up into the inner workings of the engine compartment. Billy Jean turned and met my eyes as I came into the hangar. Her expression was a mixture of alarm and warning. I took the cue and played it cool.

"Hi guys. How's it going?" I said.

"Hello, Mr. O'Keefe." Billy Jean rolled her eyes. "Long time no see. I was worried about you. We have visitors. This is Donald Long. He's a GADO inspector, and Carlos Montalbo over there is from some finance company," she said, squeezing my arm hard as if to warn me.

"Hi, glad to meet you." I shook hands with Donald Long and played dumb. "What was that inspector thing you said?"

"General Aviation District Office, GADO for short. I came over to look at this engine." He stared at me." I hear you're interested too." He was in his fifties, white hair, about 5' 10", 150 pounds, appeared unassuming and didn't mind shaking hands.

"Oh sure, I'm in the insurance investigations business. Always interested in why something like this happens," I said.

"What company do you work for?" he asked.

"I'm independent. I take cases on a contingency basis," I said.

"You on a case right now, or just killing time?" he asked.

"Don't know yet, depends," I said looking off into the distance.

"Must be nice not to know what you're doing," he said, a thin smile on his lips.

"I don't get clients by talking about their private business," I said.

"Trouble is, sometimes private business becomes public ... like this engine." He pointed up at the skeletal remains of the damaged engine on the wing above us.

"Is there something wrong here?" I asked, continuing to play dumb. Not hard to do under the circumstances.

"We'll see," he said, smiling again as he picked up a wrench and started up a ladder. "We'll see."

I turned and looked at Billy Jean who was standing beside me, a stricken look on her face. Just then the other man walked over to us.

"We should talk," he said abruptly to Billy Jean.

"Why?" I interrupted. He was about an inch shorter than me, dark skinned, black eyes, black hair, sharp features. His English was perfect with a slight inflection.

"I have business with Mrs. Furman." He glared at me. I was just about to introduce him to his ancestors when Billy Jean stepped in.

"Now let's take it easy. Bill, this is Carlos Montalbo from ... uhh ..." She searched for a name.

"Northeast Financial Services," he snarled and handed his card to me with a flourish.

"Oh, the loan sharks," I snarled back, snapping it from his hand.

"We are not loan sharks, my friend. We are a very large financial services institution and we do not have time for insurance salesmen and amateur private investigators so go away, and leave us alone!"

He put his hand on my chest and pushed. I stepped back and raised my hands palms out in a surrender mode to cool things off. The last thing I wanted was a fight with this jerk before I found out what he was up to. I wanted them to keep thinking they were in control and dealing with a scared, helpless woman and not a trained professional. It worked. He stopped pushing and smiled. Darn it! Everyone was being so damned nice, that I just naturally smiled too.

"Sure, Montalbone. You just do what you have to but let's keep it nice, okay? No sense in getting nasty," I said.

"Yes ... yes, my thoughts precisely. You understand. That is good, and it's Montalbo," he said.

He turned to Billy Jean, took her elbow and led her away under the tail of the King Air. I watched from a distance but I couldn't hear what he was saying. Billy Jean shook her head several times as he kept talking. He continued to shake her arm, and wave some papers in her face. She shook her head one last time, pulled her arm away and started yelling.

"Go to hell, you son-of-a-bitch. No way are you gonna take my business away from me, and if you hurt Tony I'll hunt you down like a dog and I'll kill you! You hear me?" she yelled.

She swung a hard right directly at his head. He blocked it and slapped her across the face. I was on him in a flash. He never knew what hit him. I caught him in the right upper rib cage with a flying kick, which sent him sprawling on his back like a rag doll across the polished hangar floor. He rolled over and tried to get up on his knees, and I drop kicked his head into the next galaxy. Then I stomped on him a couple more times just to make sure. He didn't move after that. I rolled him over and checked his pulse. He was bleeding from the mouth, nose and ears. He'd have a big headache for weeks if he lived, but I didn't care if he did. Billy Jean came over to me and I put my arms around her. We were immediately surrounded.

"What the hell ... what happened here? Why did you do that to him?" Donald Long said, suddenly becoming very official. "I'd better call the police." I grabbed his arm and stopped him.

"Why don't you wait a moment and think this over, Mr. Long." He struggled against my grip but I was bigger and stronger. "Just calm down, Donald, take it easy. Everything will be all right." He stopped struggling and glared at me.

It is amazing how people see situations, especially

fights. Seldom do they remember how it all started, only who got hurt and who won. More than one poor slob has been convicted on assault charges because some morally superior jury couldn't get it straight as to how a fight started. Much of this confusion comes out of a society that condemns any sort of violence, even self defense. Consider the case of the man convicted of murder for shooting a thief in his house. "But the thief had a gun, your Honor," said the man's lawyer.

"Doesn't matter. Your client should have run out of the house and called the police," said the judge.

Carlos had slapped Billy Jean so I suppose he should have just been slapped back, but that wasn't the point. It's not just what he did. It was what he was. He was a rotten scum-ball. His mother would have been ashamed of what he was. His priest would have condemned him. His wife would have shrunk from him and hid her face. You say, "Look, O'Keefe, perhaps you're being just a bit too hard on the man. He said he was a representative of a very large and successful financial institution, which sounds like a banker, so why did you kick the daylights out of him?" Answer is: stick around and see.

"I don't understand what you're trying to do here," said Long. "The man's a banker. Why'd you kick the hell out of him like that?"

"He hit me," blubbered Billy Jean. "Didn't you see what he did? He hit me. He threatened me and hit me and O'Keefe stepped in and stopped it." She was bleeding from her mouth and nose.

"Yeah, but you didn't have to do that to him," yelled Long.

"Let me show you something, Don," I said, letting go of his arm.

I bent down and opened Montalbo's suit coat exposing a Russian made 9mm Makarov, in a left side shoulder holster. An old but very lethal weapon. I knew it was there before, although the coat was tailored for extra space on that side. I patted him down and came up with brass knuckles (illegal), a switchblade (illegal), a ten inch stiletto from under the left pant leg (illegal), a lead weighted swatter or what Hollywood calls a blackjack, and a rolled up steel guitar string. This boy was loaded. I handed each item to General Aviation District Office Inspector Donald Long as I found them. To top it all off I found five dime packets of cocaine in his wallet and his belt buckle doubled as a slash knife.

"Now, tell me what you think, Don. What sort of banker do you think this meatball really is?" I asked.

"Good grief!" was all Don could say, his hands full of weaponry.

"Wow!" said Mickey.

"What are we going to do with the body?" Billy Jean asked.

"We could ship him down to Miami on the next flight," said one of the mechanics.

"Or Dallas," said the other mechanic.

"He's not dead yet," I said, checking his pulse.

"He will be if we don't do something," said Billy Jean.

"I shouldn't get involved in this," Donald Long said, looking around. "We should call the police and let them handle it." He was shaking all over and his eyes were bugged out.

"Listen to me, Donald!" I said. "If we call the police, they'll want to know what happened and you'll become a professional witness. Do you know what that means? Who the hell do you think this punk is, anyway? He's a criminal and that big financial company is a front that uses intimidation and strong arm tactics to make money. You want to call the police? You want to make a statement to the judge? Go ahead and see how your boss likes it when the phone calls start coming to your office threatening you if you testify. The next time he makes out your evaluation, he'll have a different idea about you. These people have ways of inflicting grievous damage on family members of witnesses too. Do you have a daughter, Donald?"

"Oh no! They wouldn't ..." He looked at me with pleading eyes and then he looked away. When he turned back he said, "They would ... ya, they would, wouldn't they!"

"You bet your life they would. These are the worst kind of criminals. They will hurt you anyway they can. Nice people don't carry stilettos and guitar strings, even if they're bankers. You know what he uses those things for? They're used to kill people," I said.

"Okay! Okay!" he said. "So, what do you want me to do?"

"I'll take care of it. He'll make it to a hospital and get what he deserves. All I want from you is an honest evaluation of that engine. Forget the rest of this and let a professional handle it," I said.

"So, I do my job and you do yours, whatever that is," said Long. He was still shaking all over and sweat dripped from his forehead.

"Right!" I took the weapons from him and watched him walk away back to the busted engine.

"What are you going to do?" asked Mickey.

"Just go back to work, son. If anyone asks, you didn't see anything and you don't know who I am. Tell the others the same thing so they'll keep quiet," I said.

I replaced all the weapons, took the papers he waved in Billy Jean's face and put them in my pocket. He was still breathing but I didn't have much time. He was badly injured and could die at any moment. His car was out in front of the hangar, a black Caddy convertible with cattle horns on the hood, a real banker's car. I moved it around the hangar and stuffed him in the trunk. Then I drove to the parking area, pulled a ticket from the gate machine, being careful to touch only the edges, and drove past the attendant who was preoccupied with a car leaving the lot.

I backed into a space up against the rail at the far end of the lot and dumped Montalbo against the boundary fence. Then I wiped the car clean of my prints. Someone would find him and he might reach the hospital in time to save his life … maybe. I looked around but didn't see anyone watching, so I started back to Furman Airways.

Meanwhile, the police would find his weapons, put it all together and decide that Mr. Montalbo of Northeast Financial Services was a crummy slime-ball hit man. The same conclusion I came to the first time we met.

Chapter Eight

It was 9:30 in the morning and I'd already captured three of the enemy. Not a bad day so far. If things kept going I might have a pile of bodies to dispose of by quitting time. Just kidding, folks. Actually, I really didn't feel all that great about what was happening. These guys were cheap hoods who seldom got what they deserved, but knocking them off wasn't getting me any closer to a solution of the Furman Airways problem. Tony Furman was still missing. The company's finances had been frozen, foreclosure proceedings had been started, and there were very bad dudes threatening to take over the business. I didn't have much time to find a solution to all these mysteries. The loan payment was due tomorrow, Friday, and the Certification Check by the FAA was due next Wednesday, which left little time, indeed.

I was reminded of the time Willie Monk asked me to help a friend of his. Seems he was being harassed by some young punks who were trying to start their own protection racket down in Brooklyn. Willie's friend was a kosher butcher with a well established business on Union Street. The punks were recently transplanted from a Caribbean Island south of Miami and had settled in the Bronx, and they didn't understand territorial rights.

One day when they were moving through the area

collecting money, we stopped them on a street corner and had a little discussion about international relations and squatter's rights. The international part was Domonic Cintelli, the local don who took care of all the security needs of the neighborhood and his friends, Antonio Paluchia and Rory Rawlins. The discussion lasted about thirty seconds and the guys from the Caribbean left the area, not under their own power, and never came back.

"Planning! Does it every time," said Willie. "Ya gotta have a plan."

I was thinking of how well Willie handled that situation as I took the parking stub and avoided the security cameras in the main terminal. He was right. I needed a plan. Billy Jean was anxiously waiting back at Furman Airways.

"Is it done, Bill? Is everything all right? Oh, this is horrible. He said I had to sign those papers and leave right away if I ever wanted to see Tony again. I never realized there were people like this in the world." We walked into the office and I looked at the papers.

"This is dumb. These papers would never hold up in court," I said. "Furman Airways is a corporation, which means you both have to sign to make the sale stick. Anyway, a signature gotten under duress is null and void. Of course, they probably don't seem to care what's legal."

"But what's going to happen to Tony?" she asked, crying.

"Just hang in there and don't give up. You did the right thing by not signing," I said. She calmed down and we had a cup of coffee. Then I filled her in on what I was planning.

"Listen, I have to go out for awhile, Billy. Don't use the telephone unless you have to. It might be bugged. If I call and tell you to call me back, this is the number I'll be at. Use your cell or a pay phone but not the one outside. Everything should be quiet for a while. I have to go arrange for your financing and find some security for the rest of the weekend." I gave her a kiss and she gave me a smile.

An ambulance, its lights flashing, was coming out of the lot with two police cars behind it as I came out of the hangar. I got into my Caddy and waited for them to leave. By now the bad guys would know they had opposition. I'd have to be more careful from now on. Still, I had to move around and I couldn't be looking over my shoulder everywhere I went. Three of them were out of the way for now. If I kept moving I might flush out a few more and eventually I might win the war by attrition.

I kept an eye out behind me for any tails but there were none that I could detect. I needed a plan. I needed information, and most of all I needed a backup and I didn't want anyone to know what I was doing. There was one place I could get all the information I needed, but I had to have Connie's authorization to do it and she wasn't around.

ITI, International Telex Incorporated, the corporation which owned Connie's employer, Daylight Inns, had data banks full of information that would put the FBI to shame. It was no ordinary communications company. It had information gathering capabilities in the private and government sectors and they maintained files on individuals as well as companies. I first ran across them when I worked for State Mutual Insurance. Companies will give anything to gain inside information on their clients or competition. I knew the man to contact and I knew what I needed. I only had to get the proper authorizations.

Connie's apartment was the same as we left it at three in the morning. I kept some spare clothes there and a shaving kit for quick changes. So I had a shave and shower, checked the mail for anything important as Connie had asked, boiled a pot of water and steeped a cup of Lapsang Souchong. Then I relaxed on the living room couch, with some J.S. Bach on the CD player. I closed my eyes and followed the music, sipped tea, and let my mind run loose.

Things had happened too fast. One moment I was in the warmth of my baby's arms and the next, it seemed, I was staring down the twin barrels of a shotgun in the wee hours of the morning. Since then I'd held another man's wife in my arms, subdued and captured two men, nearly killed a third, intimidated a federal employee into breaking the law, and dumped a body on public property. With a track record like that I could end up on the FBI's ten most wanted list.

Willie Monk always said, "In this business, there ain't no rest for the weary. All ya gotta do is get up in the mornin' and some jerk'll try to pick a fight with ya. So, ya got three choices: don't get up, walk away, or kick the stuffins outta the jerk. Now which of those do you think feels good?"

Willie was right. He'd done some street fighting while growing up in the Bronx and he could handle himself even in his later years when I knew him. His philosophy was simple: get the first punch in and make it the last. He knew every dirty trick in the book yet he was a man of compassion. If you were straight, that is to say if you had nothing to hide and you weren't embezzling funds, abusing your wife and kids, or engaged in any other nefarious activities, then Willie could be your best friend and the nicest guy you ever knew. He was from the old school of black and white where a man was either right or wrong. There was good and evil and you were measured by your choices and how you handled yourself.

Unfortunately, there's no longer a place in this modern world of gray shades and dark shadows for the likes of Willie Monk, and perhaps the same was true for me. It would take more than brute force to find Tony Furman and save Furman Airways. I needed information and, someone to watch things while I was out beating the bushes. This was not just a simple investigative job: it was all out war. I had to get organized and find some financing to keep Furman Airways going. Connie's apartment was empty and I felt her absence, but I had to put her out of my mind for now and concentrate.

The tea was just right, strong and sweet. The violins and cellos were dueling while the harpsichord filled in the spaces, and my mind was finally coming into sync with the rest of my systems. The day had been unsettling and it was now time to take control. I listened to the music and decided on the first few steps of a plan, and sorted out the sequence of the puzzle as best I could. Like the intricate interplay of the musical strains, this case seemed a real maze of complex and mysterious pieces that didn't make sense.

Willie Monk always said, "Don't worry if the pieces don't fit. Put everything on the table and play around wid it. Somethin'll fall into place." So I would sit back and let it happen, or as my music appreciation teacher in high school, Mrs. Latovian, used to say, "Listen to the themes. Watch how they repeat, double, triple, disappear, and reappear." So I took my time and let my brain play with it.

"Aha! That's it," said my brain. "The themes, follow the themes."

There were several themes already established: intimidation, kidnapping, violence, maybe sabotage, financial strangulation, big money, fraud, big crime and a South American connection. The bad guys had put together a pretty good piece, and if I hadn't stumbled onto it they would have succeeded in playing it out to the end by taking over Furman Airways. I intended to prevent that from happening. The first impulse was to rush out to find Tony Furman and save him but that was a false dominant theme. "Listen for a deeper and more abiding theme," my mind said. "Don't be fooled by the first thing you hear."

So, Tony Furman would wait. They would keep him alive as long as they didn't get what they wanted. I would play the financial theme first. My ex-father-in-law, Jack Sullivan, owed me a favor. He was a retired banker with a lot of financial savvy and I had saved his entire fortune from unscrupulous investors. He loved flying and had an airstrip on the hill behind his estate overlooking the Hudson River in upper Westchester County. I dialed his number, took a big gulp of tea, turned the stereo down, and on the third ring he answered.

"Jack!" I said. "How would you like to own an airline?"

"I already own one," he answered.

"Not like this one ..." I said, and I filled him in. Before I was half done he was hooked.

"I'll finish up here and fire up the twin Beech. I'll be down right after lunch," he said.

Backup number one was on the way. I left a message for Deputy Sheriff Kim Woo to call me. Ten minutes later he did.

"Man, I've been trying to find you, O'Keefe. I don't know what you've gotten into but it must be big, real big!" he said.

"Why do you say that? What have you got for me?" I asked.

"Nothing! That's just the point. I had to appear in court this morning so I took those two goons down to the courthouse and stuck them in a holding cell. They never said a word, just followed along like two lost sheep. I told the bailiff to watch them until I finished testifying and I would be down to pick them up. I was going to take them over to the station in town and do some pictures and fingerprints like I was having them booked, you know, like you asked me, but when I came down from court, they were gone," he said.

"What? Did they break out?" I asked.

"They didn't have to. The bailiff let them make a phone call. One of them said he had to call his boss or he would lose his job. Next thing the bailiff knows, this high-priced lawyer shows up with papers to release these guys and they're gone. So help me, O'Keefe, they were like ghosts. I never got an ID on them or a picture or anything. It's like it never happened," Kim said.

"Any idea who the lawyer was?" I asked.

"Oh, yeah! Man, now this is where it gets interesting. First of all, tell me this. What did you do with their car?"

"I left it right there with the keys on the front seat," I said.

"Right," Kim said. "Well, seems they went back there to retrieve their car and it was gone. So, there I am back in court testifying and in walks this high-priced lawyer. He slams the doors open, bangs the gate aside and walks right up to Judge Shirley Lipsitts. I'm testifying about how this hubby comes home and finds his wife in bed with his boss and takes a baseball bat to the two of them, and Mr. High-Priced lawyer demands to know where I am and where's the car and who the hell did I think I was, beating up on his poor innocent little boys?"

"You mean he interrupted the trial? I bet the judge loved that!"

"I thought Judge Lipsitts would have a bird," said Woo, "but she didn't. She has a reputation for being a real man-eater but she just looked surprised, got real red in the face and then, by God, she apologized to this jerk lawyer. Can you believe it? She said she was sorry for any inconvenience and what could she do to help. She knew who he was, some big deal New York attorney, Morton Bolinsky. Ever hear of him?"

"Yeah. I don't know much about him, just what I read in the newspapers. He does a lot of drug cases," I said.

"More than that. I did some research on him. He is 'Mr. Big'. He handles all the big drug cartel business and he's got clout, as you can tell by the way Judge Lipsitts behaved. I had to apologize all over hell for apprehending his two little boys. Man was he ticked. My boss is on my case and I'll be lucky if I don't end up as a crossing guard down at the elementary school. I want to really thank you for giving me the opportunity to meet these wonderful people, O'Keefe. Next time you decide to rattle someone's cage, don't call me. I'm not qualified to handle Mr. Big with drug connections to Bogota. I'll leave that privilege in your capable hands," he said.

"You really are rattled, aren't you? Honest, Kim, I had no idea who those guys were. I just took a chance that you were in the area. I'm as surprised as you are, but now that I know about this Morton Bolinsky, I'll be more careful. You can bet on that. Yeah, I guess that about does it. Thanks. Now I'll need to find someone else with the right qualifications to help me out on this case. Someone with cool, steady nerves, who doesn't get easily rattled over a little thing like a Colombian drug cartel or kidnapping and extortion and maybe attempted murder. I guess I'll have to find a real law enforcement officer with experience to back me up. I'll even pay double."

"Okay! Okay, enough already. What do you want, O'Keefe?"

"I thought you would never ask," I said.

I told him about Furman Airways. I explained the way they put the squeeze on Billy Jean, about Tony's disappearance, the engine explosion, and Carlos Montalbo. I told him about my ex-father-in-law, Jack Sullivan, and the need to find Tony Furman before the FAA certification check came the following Wednesday.

"You're running a tight schedule but you got my interest," he said. "Besides, I don't like being pushed around by high-priced lawyers and drug dealers. I've got some time off coming and my boss will probably not object, so count me in."

I told him to be at the airport before dark, to come armed and ready for action, and to be prepared to stay awhile. I remembered after I hung up that I didn't tell him about the boxes of roots in the back of the Ford sedan, but I still had the one I took from the trunk.

Kim Woo was a very unusual young man, in his early thirties. I met him the previous year while on a case that involved Jack Sullivan and other very important people. He worked as a deputy sheriff in Westchester County just north of New York City. A second generation Korean-American, born in this country shortly after his parents arrived. He spent time around the Mediterranean as an Air Force intelligence officer. He also had assignments in Afghanistan, Angola, Nicaragua, Beirut and Somalia. He had a voracious intellect and a memory for details that amazed me.

When my children were kidnapped he risked his life and job to help me. We stood shoulder to shoulder under fire and he never flinched. I asked him once why he didn't try out for the CIA or FBI and he just shrugged and said, "I had enough of that already. What I do now gives me time to do what I enjoy most." So, I asked him what that was and he just smiled and said, "To be myself," and I thought, "Yeah, that works for me."

The tea was cold, the Bach was finished, I was shaved, showered, had a fresh set of clothes, and it was time for work. The ball was rolling and I was ready to start beating the bushes. The telephone rang as I washed my teacup. I answered it and found Connie on the line. She was at the hospital near her family home in Wilson, Iowa. She said her father was no longer critical. He had been upgraded to a guarded prognosis and everyone was anxiously waiting. The doctors said the heart attack was massive and there would be damage.

She was very upset, not just about her father's condition but also about the way she had left me standing on the tarmac at the airport. I reassured her I was all right and would be waiting for her when she returned. She was pleased with that. I could tell that it had all been too quick for her too. Then she asked me what I was doing and I told her: drinking tea, listening to J.S. Bach, and working on this problem a friend has over at Furman Airways. She was interested but couldn't talk under the circumstances.

"I'm standing out here in a hallway at a public telephone with people sitting all around me. I wish it were more private," she said.

"It's just good to hear your voice. I hope your Dad pulls through. I'm sorry this happened. Is there anything I can do for you?" What could I say in a situation like this?

"Thanks, Bill. Now that I'm here I suppose things will look better. I just had to call to see if you were okay. By the way, is there anything you need?"

"I'm working on this sort-of case and I need some information. Would it be all right if I used your computer? I don't want to cause any trouble but it would just make things easier if I could do my research here. Also, I may need to call Chicago."

"Oh sure, no problem. I told my boss you would be around to keep an eye on things. I guess you'll need my code. You'll never guess what it is. I only changed it last week. It's 'WILLIE'. Surprised? I knew you would never guess the old one so I changed it." She was a smart girl.

We reaffirmed our love, said our goodbyes, and hung up. I wanted to return to the airport before Jack Sullivan arrived but I didn't make it. Jack's twin Beech was on the apron outside the Furman hangar when I drove in and he was in the office with Billy Jean.

"This could be a real good deal, Mr. Sullivan, if we find Tony and get him back in the driver's seat before the FAA check next week," said Billy Jean as I walked in. "Oh, Bill, you didn't tell me Mr. Sullivan was coming, but I'm glad he did."

"I was just going over the books and talking possibilities with Mrs. Furman," said Jack, a gleam in his eye. He turned to Billy Jean. "How much is the monthly payment that's due tomorrow?"

"It's there in the papers," she answered. "It's over $30,000. The interest rate is fourteen something. Oh, I don't know all this stuff. It's an awful amount of money. Tony takes care of this end of the business. They froze our assets with the foreclosure notice so I can't get at the money, and there seems to be a blacklisting on our business because no other bank will even talk to us. That's really not legal is it, Mr. Sullivan?" Billy Jean asked.

"As an ex-banker, Mrs. Furman, I can tell you it is not what is legal, it's how things are done. Unscrupulous people are victimizing you and they know you can't last long. Even if I bankroll the business, they may succeed in sabotaging it in other ways. We have to find out who they are and stop them. I can tell you from personal experience that O'Keefe is the one who can do that for you. So, if you are willing, I'll put up the cash and we'll go from there," he said.

"I don't know what to say. I guess ... well ... yes, of course, but what do you want in return, Mr. Sullivan?" she asked. "I can't let you take over Furman Airways. Tony would never stand for it."

"Just pay me back," Jack said with a banker's smile.

Chapter Nine

WE sent out for Chinese food and that's as exciting as it got until Jimmy Linn stuck his head inside the office and said, "Linda's coming in."
"Any problems?" asked his mother.
"No, but she's an hour late. Just thought you'd like to know."
"Thanks, I was wondering where she was," said Billy Jean.

We heard the sound of the aircraft coming toward the hangar, the whine of the turbines masked by the roar of the props. Suddenly the steady sound of the props changed to a deafening roar and Billy Jean bolted from her chair. Jack and I followed her out of the office and through the hangar. Mickey and Jimmy Linn were ahead of us, each trailing wheel chocks in their hands.

The King Air was rolling toward a line of parked aircraft and it appeared that it wouldn't stop in time to avoid a collision even with the props in full reverse. Mickey suddenly took a flying dive under the right wing, landed on his belly and expertly swung a wheel chock by its rope under the right front main wheel. One edge of the triangular wooden block caught under the rolling wheel and for a moment it seemed as if it might bounce loose when Jimmy Linn came up under the tail and jammed his chock under the left main wheel. Linda feathered the props and cut the engines. The rest of us waited as Billy Jean let down the stairway and started up into the cabin of the aircraft.

"Linda!" shouted her mother. "Are you all right?"

"Yeah, just lost my brakes," came the answer in a voice much like her mother's.

Billy Jean went forward into the airplane and I was tempted to follow when something odd struck me. Call it a freak intuition. Call it an old warrior's paranoia, whatever. I looked around and saw that everyone was there. Billy Jean was on board the aircraft with Linda. Mickey and Jimmy Linn were working around the left main landing gear, looking up into the wheel well of the wing. The two extra mechanics and inspector Donald Long were standing right there behind Jack and me. The gang was all there and no one, I say again no one, was in the hangar. "So, what's the problem, O'Keefe?" said a little voice in the back of my brain. "Simple," I mumbled back. I would swear I saw a movement inside the hangar out of the corner of my eye,"

"Jack! Follow me," I yelled as I ran for the hangar. He was right behind me when we reached the entrance. We were hidden by the airplanes and equipment jammed inside and I laid down on the floor. At first I saw nothing, and I was beginning to feel foolish. Then I noticed a pant leg next to an airplane behind one of the smaller aircraft on the far side of the hangar.

"Over there," I whispered to Jack and pointed. He squinted but shook his head.

"I don't see anyone," he said.

"Go into the office and make sure nobody gets in there. I'll circle around, grab this one and see what he's up to," I whispered.

I crept off toward the back wall of the hangar, keeping myself hidden from the intruder. I came within twenty feet and found cover behind a water cooler where I could watch him. There was a space alongside a King Air where I would have no cover, but I couldn't see any other way to go. I considered rushing across the opening, and was just about to start my attack when there was a shout and a bang behind me. The intruder, who was turned away from me, his head stuck in the open cowling of the airplane, suddenly turned and looked in the direction of the office.

He was a short man with dark skin, long wavy hair and thick bifocals hanging off his nose. There was a striking similarity to Carlos Montalbo, but in a miniaturized version. He turned and looked under the cowling again. The ruckus in the office had now turned into a full-fledged fight. I could hear the grunts, the groans, and the familiar smacking of fists against flesh. I was just starting to move when he turned again and I tried to pull up. He caught the movement out of the side of his vision and turned round facing me, so I charged.

Well folks, it never fails that something will go wrong. No matter how many times you practice something, no matter how many dry runs you make or how many times you run through a plan, something will go wrong. In the military they call it "poor planning" and the worst thing you can say to a leader of men, next to calling the fellow a coward, is to say he is guilty of "poor planning".

You can say a man made an error in judgment. You can even say he is an arrogant, bull-headed SOB, but that is nothing next to saying he engaged in "poor planning". You might as well call him lazy and stupid. So there I was making my move to grab this fellow and I slipped on the highly polished floor and fell splat right flat on my face! See what I mean? Poor planning!

Tony and Billy Jean ran a sharp, clean outfit. The cement floor of the hangar was finished with a special oil resistant high gloss poly-sealing wax so oil or gas leaks would be found immediately and wouldn't sink into the concrete floor. The spot where I was kneeling was not well traveled and was even more slippery. So there I was trying to get up and get going and my quarry took off running. I saw it all as I lay on the floor. He rounded the nose of the King Air, ducked under the right wing and tried a sharp left turn around the tail of the next airplane Then he slipped on the nice clean polished floor and crashed unceremoniously into a big red tool chest on rollers, knocked over a work stand next to the tool chest and bounced off the back workbench.

I was up on all fours by this time and was certain I had him. He pulled himself up using the workbench, and crashed out of the emergency exit, triggering the alarm as he went. I made it to the door in time to see him climb into the passenger side of a plain dark blue Ford with tinted windows, similar to the brown one that tailed me just that morning. The driver floored it, leaving about fifty feet of rubber and disappeared down the road and onto the highway with a roar. The alarm was deafening, and I was tempted to smash the darn thing with a hammer when Billy Jean showed up with a set of keys and turned it off.

"What's wrong with you, O'Keefe, can't you read? The big red sign says 'EMERGENCY EXIT' - 'ALARM'," she yelled.

"Just stupid, I guess." I replied. I waited as she closed the door and reset the alarm. "I have something for you to look at," I said. "By the way, what was all the noise in the office? Is Jack okay?"

"Yes, he caught somebody in the office," she said. "Where were you?"

I took her to the Aerostar with the open cowling and described the man I saw working on the engine. I showed her where he fell and the work stand he knocked over. That's where we found his glasses, smashed under the work stand. I described how he'd gone out the emergency door and escaped in the souped up Ford.

"Riccardo Fernandes," said Billy Jean. "He took flying lessons here until we caught him going through the files in the office."

"When was that?" I asked.

"Last month sometime ..." She thought a moment. "Yes, it was three weeks ago. Tony was very upset. There didn't seem to be anything missing but the very idea that someone we trusted was rifling through our files really upset him." We walked to the airplane and Billy Jean looked inside the open cowling.

"Oh no," she exclaimed, "look at this," she pointed.

She reached inside and pulled out a small aluminum cylinder about an inch long, stuck in a ball of putty with two wires, one green and the other yellow, still attached to a cable running down the firewall of the engine compartment. I grabbed her hand and held it steady.

"Don't move, Sweetheart. That's a bomb you're holding in your hand. Just let me have it and back out of the way." She did as I said.

I traced the wiring and saw that both leads were firmly attached to the electric motor that operated the nose gear. I carefully pulled the blasting cap out of the plastic and handed the ball of high explosive to Billy Jean.

"I thought you said this was a bomb," said Billy Jean, "so why are you giving it to me? Don't you love me anymore?"

"Of course, I'll always love you, Billy Jean. Don't worry, that's plastic explosive and it's harmless without a detonator. You can throw it, burn it, eat it, flush it down the toilet, and even let your kids play with it. This blasting cap is attached to the nose gear motor, so when you take off and pull the gear lever up everything goes boom."

"That ball of explosive was up against this firewall, wrapped around the fuel line and next to an oil line. Blow a hole in the firewall, sever the fuel line and dump some oil into it and the cabin becomes a fiery, smoky, nightmare." I pointed to the spot where some of the putty-like explosive was still clinging to the lines. "That boy, Riccardo, is a real dream maker. Tell me, who uses this airplane?" I asked.

"This is our IFR trainer used for instrument training. It's an older plane, so it's not used as much," she said.

"Who is scheduled to use it next?" I asked.

"Actually, no one. The next time it would go up

is Wednesday when the FAA inspector comes for the annual certification check. I would be the pilot on that check ride if Tony isn't here," she said.

"You'd be the dead pilot along with the inspector. These people mean business. We've got to tighten security," I said.

"Speaking of which," said Billy Jean, "Jack caught someone in the office messing around with the lights. They had a real battle before Jack subdued him. The office is a mess."

"How's Jack? Did he get banged up?"

"I don't know. He looked all right but I didn't have time to chat. I had to turn off the emergency alarm on the back door." She gave me a sheepish grin. "Sorry about that remark."

"It's okay. You didn't know," I said.

We found everyone cleaning up the office. I was introduced to Linda, and the surprise must have shown on my face. This was not the young girl I remembered from seven years before. She was taller than her mother with a slim attractive figure, short brown hair, the same big brown eyes her mother possessed and a smile that would set a young man's heart on fire, or an old man's - whichever you happened to be. Jack was banged up a bit but his spirits were high.

"I caught this jasper messing with the light switch. I had a job of it trying to get him under control but I finally managed. I tied him up with the telephone cord," he said.

The intruder was lying face down on the floor, his hands and feet tied behind him. I rolled him over and he tried to kick me with his feet even though they were tied. He was dark skinned with black hair and Latino features. Another soldier from the enemy camp.

"Try that again Poncho, and I'll separate your head from your body," I snarled, picking him up by the hair of his head. "You understand me?" He didn't say anything. "Blink your eyes if you want to live, jerk." He blinked.

"Ask him what he was doing," said Billy Jean.

I ask him but he refused to answer. I let go of his hair and watched his face slam hard on the cement floor. "Take him out into the hangar and watch him so we can talk," I said to Mickey.

I walked over to the wall switch with its open faceplate and examined it. A pair of wires was connected through the back of the box and ran up the backside of the conduit that led to the fluorescent lamp overhead. A strip of tape the same color as the wall cleverly concealed the extra set of wires. The ceiling was at least twelve feet high but the light fixture hung down to about the seven-foot level, making for a dark space above the light. The wires led to a little black box in the corner up in the darkened area. I climbed up on a file cabinet and retrieved the box, unplugged the wires, and brought it down. It was about a foot square and had a hole in the side. I opened the latch and found a miniature camcorder inside.

"Looks like they were trying to find out what we're up to. I would say we got them worried. This is no ordinary camera," I said.

I plugged it in a wall socket and waved my hand in front of the opening. The recording light blinked on and the camera very quietly began to record. "I've read about these. A company out in California takes a basic stock camera and turns it into a surveillance unit capable of recording for a forty-eight-hour period. With the motion detector the recording time can be stretched over a longer period, like several days or more. Just sneak in and change the CD and you're in the spy business."

"But why put that thing in here now? They've already frozen our bank accounts and Tony's gone. Why start spying on us now?" Billy Jean asked.

"Because, my dear lady, the situation has changed. Some mysterious hired guns have come to town and the bad guys are worried. They want to know who I am and who this old geezer is." I pointed to Jack. "They want to know what happened to their head killer, Carlos Montalbo, and why you're still in business. They may not be scared but they're definitely worried. That bomb in the instrument trainer, now that was a real desperation move. If they were really sure of themselves they would just wait until you can't make it any longer, but no, they can't wait. They're operating on a short fuse, which makes them more dangerous," I said.

"You can say that again," said Mickey, walking into the office. "The brake lines on Linda's airplane were sabotaged. They had very small manmade cuts that slowly bled the brakes on both sides."

"But how did that happen?" asked Linda, her eyes widening. "I never left the aircraft ... well maybe I did, now that I think of it...on the ground in Newark ..." She looked around the room. "Well, it was a long flight!" she said, and we all laughed.

Billy Jean said, "Linda, doesn't know what's going on. I didn't tell her because I wasn't sure, and besides, she's been gone for two days. The Dallas-Houston run is a long flight and it requires an overnight."

"What is it, Mother? What's wrong?" asked Linda.

"I ... uhh ..." Billy Jean looked down and began to cry.

"Linda," I said. "Your mother has been under a great deal of stress. Someone is trying to take over Furman Airways. They've frozen the company's bank accounts, served foreclosure papers, and evidently kidnapped your father. Now it appears they're trying to sabotage the company's aircraft."

"Oh no!" Linda exclaimed as she went to Billy Jean and put her arms around her. "Why didn't you tell me?"

"I don't think she knew what to do," I said. "It's a dirty business and no one is equipped to deal with this sort of pressure: extortion, kidnapping, fraud, and attempted murder. There's no manual available at your local bookstore that tells you what to do if international drug criminals decide to put the cattle prod to your business, kidnap your chief pilot, and close down your bank accounts. It's not like following a pre-flight checklist or an IFR flight plan. When the bad guys come knocking, there are no rules."

"This is hard to believe," said Jimmy Linn. "There have to be laws against this. How can they just walk in and throw us out and then steal our business? Somebody should do something."

"Somebody is doing something," I said.

Inspector Donald Long came into the office and

looked around. He glanced back at the man on the floor in the hangar and looked at me with a questioning expression.

"Hi Don," I said, trying to keep it light. "We caught that one messing around in the office. What can I do for you?"

"I'm not sure," he said. "I think maybe I should be on my way to the FBI right now but they probably wouldn't believe it." He pulled his right hand out of his overalls and produced two small wires, yellow and green. I recognized them right away.

"We found these connected to a small pencil-sized flashlight up near the engine struts in the wing of Jimmy Linn's airplane. The flashlight was smashed against a structural baffle. At first I thought some sloppy mechanic left it there but then I found these wires. Any idea what they are?"

"Yes." I pulled the blasting cap, out of my pocket and showed it to him. It had the same colored wires, about twenty inches long. "Recognize this?" I asked.

"Wow! It's a blasting cap, but where did you get it?" He asked.

I explained about the instrument flight trainer and the intruder I caught working under the cowling, and how we found the bomb rigged to the nose gear motor. I showed him the gray putty-like plastik, which I had in my other pocket, and gave him my theory about how it was supposed to work, essentially creating a fireball with smoke in the cockpit. Then I told him about the flight check and Tony Furman and the attempt by some unknown bad guys to take over Furman Airways.

"Now you are up to date. I only came into it this morning. Now that you've confirmed sabotage on Jimmy Linn's airplane, I can move ahead on tracking these people down," I said.

"I don't know about that, Mr. O'Keefe. I'm required to turn over anything like this to the FBI," said Long. "Besides, I'm the one who would probably have drawn that flight check next Wednesday and that means I would have been in that cockpit when the fireball struck. I can tell you that scares the hell out of me."

"Look, Don, I can't keep you from calling the FBI and right now I guess it might be a good thing. But I'm afraid we'll scare them away, and I want to get the people who are really behind this, the big guys and their henchmen. They'll just step back into the murky shadows of the international criminal world and we'll never be able to prove anything. We may even lose Tony Furman and I don't want that to happen," I said.

"But the FBI has men, money, endless resources. They have the power to do things. Why don't you want them to help you?" he said.

"Maybe I can help here," said Jack Sullivan. "I've seen the FBI at work, and they're good. They have unlimited resources, but there are things the FBI cannot do with criminals like these. O'Keefe does those things better than anyone else. Remember last year, a group of terrorists killed that helicopter pilot up at Croton-on-Hudson?"

"That was Jerry Warren, Kenny's brother, a good friend of mine," said Long.

"Well," said Jack. "This is the man who tracked them down and put an end to it all."

"Holy shit!" muttered Long, his eyes wide in an expression of total surprise. "I should have known."

"Let me put it this way," Jack continued. "When you find rats in your pantry who do you call, the FBI?"

"No, I suppose you would call an exterminator," said Long.

"Right," said Jack. "Well, let me introduce you to the exterminator: William Thackery O'Keefe." No one laughed.

Chapter Ten

JACK Sullivan was laying it on pretty thick, but he was right. The FBI would do a far superior job in many ways. After a lengthy and thorough investigation they would go to the Department of Justice, who, if convinced of the merits of the case, would go to a grand jury to seek indictments. If those indictments were approved, there would be warrants issued for the arrest of somebody connected with the whole affair, and sometime within the next year or more there would or might be a hearing in a courtroom to determine if the suspect should be tried on that or related charges.

At this point some sharp, highly paid big-gun attorney would seek a plea bargain and a deal would be struck to reduce the charges or let the bad guys go free in return for information on other criminals the government is more interested in prosecuting. Meanwhile, Furman Airways and the rights of its owners and employees would become secondary to the judicial process and the professional interests of a multitude of career minded civil servants. Too pessimistic? Try getting raped or mugged and then give me a call. I think you may change your mind.

One of the mechanics came into the office. "Man, what a mess. I'm finding pieces of junk in that engine that I can't identify. Tell me if you know what this is." He held up what appeared to be half of a clock face. "It's got numbers on it and look, there's still a piece of glass in the edge." He pointed to a burned piece of metal.

"Let me see that," said Donald Long. He examined it in the light of the window. "Where was this?" He handed it to Billy Jean.

"Back in the engine cowling near the wing strut, not far from where we found that little flashlight. What do you think it is?" asked the mechanic. We all examined it closely.

"It's part of an old altimeter face. Yes, that's what it is," said Jack. "There, see that? That's where a spring-loaded diaphragm was attached. This is really old, like the ones they used to have in the old Piper J-3 Cubs back in the 1940's, but what's it doing in the wing of a modern King Air?"

"Pressure detonated bomb," I said. "Jimmy Linn, you said you were climbing through 10,200 feet when the engine blew up, right?" He agreed. "If you hadn't been held down by incoming traffic from the north when you departed Boston, you would have been in the clouds, IFR, in a climbing configuration over a congested area when it blew. The worst possible place."

"It certainly sounds like a pressure activated bomb," said Billy Jean. "You're lucky it didn't do more damage. There's a gas tank right next to that engine pod in the wing."

"The reason it didn't do more damage," said Long, "is because of the way the aircraft is built. There's a requirement that a baffle or firewall be installed between any gas tank and engine compartment. That firewall is designed to withstand the worst possible disaster which would be a crash combined with engine explosion and fire."

"So, what you're saying is, whoever put that bomb in there didn't know what he was doing?" I asked. "That if he had known how the aircraft was constructed he would have done a better job?"

"That's probably true," said Long. "These aircraft are built to withstand ten times the stress normally encountered in routine flight operations. People have no idea of the effort and care that goes into building an airplane. That's what makes them so expensive."

"One thing's for sure," said Mickey, "it's going to take a long time and a lot of money to fix that airplane. I can fix the brake lines on Linda's airplane tonight, but the engine on Jimmy Linn's King Air is gone, too much damage. We can't afford it, Mom."

"What if you had no money problems?" asked Jack. "How long would it take you to fix that aircraft?"

"Working around the clock? Maybe two or three days, if I can keep these extra mechanics and if the FAA will inspect and certify the work. That's always a holdup. Then there's getting the engine from Engine Reworks in Wichita," Mickey said.

"No problem on the engine," said Billy Jean. "I already called Wichita, and you can keep the two mechanics."

"I'll stick close and certify the work," said Long.

"I'll see to it you have the necessary funds," said Jack.

"I can pick up the engine tomorrow night on my next Dallas-Houston run," said Linda.

"I'll take the Aero Commander on my next Miami run," said Jimmy Linn.

"I'll work around the clock starting right now," said Mickey.

"Management by participation," said Jack. "Always works."

"I'll dispose of this stiff," I said. "Nice to be part of a team effort."

Actually, I wasn't going to dispose of the man, as in bury him or toss him out along the highway. I brought my car around, used a coil of nylon clothesline to retie his hands and feet, and dumped him into my trunk. Billy Jean was getting ready for a flight to Montreal. I told her to expect Kim Woo to arrive later. I borrowed one of her handheld radios, got Jack in the passenger's seat of my Caddy, and drove to Connie's apartment where I parked in a dark corner of the underground Executive Parking Area to avoid the security cameras.

I untied my prisoner's feet, stood him up, and walked him to the elevator, being certain to keep his tied hands hidden from the cameras by my body. The elevator required an access code, which Connie had given me, and the door opened directly into a private corridor leading to her corner of the building. We were lucky no one was around and we made it to the apartment without being seen.

"I'm putting this fellow in your care," Jack. "He's got no ID, he won't talk, and he thinks he's a tough guy so I'm turning him over to you for interrogation and reprogramming. All I ask is that you don't kill him. I want that pleasure for myself," I said, turning my back to the prisoner and giving Jack a wink.

"You always have the fun while I do all the work," said Jack, repressing a smile. "Can I torture him just a little?"

"Have your fun but leave the good part for me," I said.

The man looked stricken as Jack led him into the bedroom and tied him to the bedpost. I put some water in the kettle and heated it for tea, found a couple of cans of chili con carne, a box of Carolina brown rice, and a can of peas. There was no cheese. Well, you can't have it all. I whipped up a gourmet chili lover's meal, added a couple of Mexican beers, and called Jack from the bedroom.

"Chili con carne on a bed of brown rice, with green peas? Yuck!" said Jack. "I don't believe you did that, Billy. Green peas on the same plate with chili and rice? If my grandmother, Matty O'Sullivan, ever saw this she would disown me for even sitting down at the same table with you."

"Stop your complaining and eat, you old fart. Your grandmother's name was Mary and she loved green peas," I said.

"You're just saying that so I'll eat the darn things. You know I hate green peas. I refuse to eat them," he said, pushing back from the table. "I don't care if my dear departed grandmother liked them or not, I can't eat them. They turn my stomach. Give them to the fellow in the bedroom. He'll probably confess at the mere sight of the first plate full of green peas. Just the very thought of being forced to eat them will make him talk."

"Eat your chili, Jack. You'll need all the energy you can find to get through the interrogation sessions you're about to conduct. Do you understand me, Igor?" I mimicked the mad scientist.

"I see," said Jack, picking up the mad scientist routine. "When will we remove the prisoner's brain for the transplant operation? I want to be sure I have enough staples in my staple gun for the procedure," he laughed. "But really, Bill, what am I supposed to do? I'm a banker, not an interrogator. What do you expect of me?"

"Jack, has it ever occurred to you that bankers are probably the best interrogators in the world and nobody can persecute a man like a banker can? This fellow is just a peon but he may be able to point us in the right direction. Do whatever you can to make him talk, but be careful. It's easy to go overboard. The line between interrogation and torture can be very thin. Once you cross it you may find you've lost control. That's why many prisoners die under so-called questioning. Some interrogators don't know when to stop," I said.

"You're scaring me. Maybe I shouldn't do this." he said.

"No, I want you to be cautious. I just want him to talk and you can make him do it. Use your own judgment but remember these are not Sunday school teachers. They're kidnappers, blackmailers, and murderers. Don't take any chances. Always keep his hands and feet tied. I don't care if you have to change his diapers. Do not, I repeat, do not let him loose for any reason!" I said.

"Okay, okay! I've got it," Jack said, shoveling a big spoonful of chili and rice into his mouth. "I was in the Navy long before you even knew what a diaper was. They taught us how to take prisoners and how to watch them. I think I can remember most of that and I might even enjoy it. Go do what you have to. I'll get the dishes. We don't want to leave Connie any messes."

"Okay, Jack, but there's one more thing," I said.

"What's that?"

"Can I have the rest of your green peas?"

He scooped up a spoonful of peas and winged them at me. Caught me right in the left eye. "Thanks, that was really good," I said.

It was serious research time, so while Jack watched the prisoner I fired up Connie's computer terminal, entered her code, "WILLIE", and began searching. I tapped into the company's credit files using Connie's access manual and checked the histories of Carlos Montalbo and Riccardo Fernandes and drew blanks. I tried several other sources and got the same results. I tried Morton Bolinsky and got blocked. There was a computer lockout on his name, so I picked up the phone and dialed an old friend in Chicago. John Chusak answered on the second ring. He was Director of Security for American Telex International, one of the parent corporations that owned Connie's company, Daylight Inns.

"O'Keefe, you old beggar. Connie told us you would be using her apartment while she was away. Sorry to hear about her father. What's up? You chasing bad guys again?" he said.

"Always, Johnny. I got locked out on a name in the computer, Morton Bolinsky. Can you help me?" I asked.

"Yeah, let me see what I got. Old Mort is heavy stuff. We protect our files on guys like this. The information can get a man killed," he said.

"Nice," I echoed.

"Yeah, here it is," he said. "Morton Bolinsky was born Mariano Julio Bolinsky in Buenaventura, Colombia, a small town on the northern coast. His father was a Romanian immigrant who made whoopy with the daughter of a local plantation owner. There were no marriage papers. As a boy, he showed promise in his studies and was sent to the good old U.S.A. to attend private schools, and eventually attended Harvard Law School. All this was funded by a combination of monies from the plantation and profits earned from a drug export business developed by his brother, Rudolfo Bolinsky. He entered the practice of law in New York City and quickly became famous for his defense of drug pushers and junkies. If you got busted, call Morton. His phone number is scrawled on the walls of toilets and drug dens all over the greater metropolitan area, including half of Jersey and Connecticut. He lives on Long Island, out in the Hamptons in one of the old estates once owned by a robber baron," he said.

"How good is this information, John? Is it something I can confirm or just some stoolie's gossip bought for a couple of beers?"

"This is good stuff. We pay for it and then we double-check it by selling it to people like you, but it's free because you're Connie's friend," he said.

"So, you buy this information and put it in your data banks for anyone who wants it and can pay for it?" I said.

"Not quite. Not just anyone can use it. For instance, we've had two inquires just this morning from the FBI and one from the CIA, not to mention all the background checks we do for corporations and municipalities. We charge fifty dollars a name and warn our clients to be careful with what we give them. If something proves untrue, we ask they notify us so we can correct our records. If it's something really big, we refund the fee to the client and go back to the source to take corrective action," John said.

"So, you're telling me people sent you this info on Morton Bolinsky and got paid for it, and if I find it's not true, you'll pay me to correct it?"

"Yes," Chusak said. "A desk sergeant in a precinct in Houston, Texas submitted part of this report. We paid him twenty-five dollars for it. Another portion comes from a DEA agent in Miami. That's one of the reasons we're very careful who we give it to. They could get killed for passing information like this around."

"But isn't it illegal to sell confidential government information?"

"Yes, but then the same agencies turn around and buy it back from us," said John. "We sell a lot of information to the insurance industry. They can't get enough. It' a very lucrative business and it's not controlled by the government. The legality of it is vague but as long as you don't hurt anyone it works out. If we dealt just in credit reporting we would have to be very careful, but personal background checks are a wide open area and we would like to keep it that way."

"I can well imagine you would. So, tell me John, is there anything else I need to know about Mr. Bolinsky?"

"Yes there is, and this is the part you'd better keep under your hat. Even though Morton Bolinsky was born in Colombia, he managed somehow to have his birth recorded in New York City so he appears to be a native born citizen of the U.S.A. I suppose all it takes is a little clout, a few bucks, and you can buy your way into the record books. He is very sensitive about this and only a few very close friends know about it. Not even the FBI knows. The drug lords in Colombia don't know. It's new information and you're the first to hear it," he said.

"Ahh, so Mr. Respectable-Harvard-Law-School Bolinsky from New York City is really the bastard son of a murky Colombian liaison," I said.

"Yes, and it's said that Bolinsky would kill to protect that information. By the way, there's a note here that he is responsible for ordering the murders of several prominent crime figures during the past year, trying to take over their businesses. He's ruthless and he's getting bigger by the minute, so be careful," John said.

"How about friends and relatives? Who are the people he travels with? Got anything on that?" I asked.

"Yes, I'll send them along. Just turn on your fax," said John.

"Also, I need rundowns on North East Financial Services in New York City, Bryn Mawr Bank and Trust Company, and two additional names: Carlos Montalbo and Riccardo Fernandes."

"Yeah, sure, but you better be very careful, my friend. Carlos Montalbo is a real tough character. He's an assassin and had to leave Colombia because of the heat. He killed two judges, a police chief, and a bunch more prominent people who got in the way of the drug cartels. They say he's a walking arsenal."

"I have an update for your records, John. Carlos Montalbo walked into a meat grinder this afternoon. He should be listed, right now, in fair to poor condition in the Westchester County Hospital and under police guard. Like you say, I am always careful, and you don't have to pay me for this update," I said.

"Does Morton Bolinsky know about this?" asked Chusak.

"I don't know and I don't care," I said. "Why?"

"Because," said John, "Carlos Montalbo is Morton Bolinsky's half brother. Same father, different mother but they are very close. You better find a real deep hole to hide in, because when Morton Bolinsky finds out what you've done he'll send everyone he has after you."

Chapter Eleven

THE dishes were finished and I went to the bedroom to check on Jack. He was sitting cross-legged on the floor, facing the man and talking in Spanish.

"My Spanish is classical. Learned it in Spain, running with the bulls in Pamplona. This fellow speaks a South American version. He speaks some English too but not much, so I think we'll get along." Jack said.

"Well, that's a start. If you get anything, let me know," I said.

"He wants to know if we are going to kill him. If so, he would like to speak to a priest. He says that is the only thing he asks."

"Tell him it all depends on him. If he cooperates, we'll let him live. Tell him if he doesn't cooperate, I'll turn him into a eunuch, comprende?" I looked at the man and saw him visibly react to my words.

I left Jack to his interrogations and returned to the corner of the living room where Connie had her office setup. The fax was churning out paper and I found several surprises. I examined the face in the picture as each report came off the machine. They were all there. Riccardo Fernandes with the thick glasses turned out to be a cousin of Morton Bolinsky with an address in Southold on Long Island, not too far from my own cottage in the sand dunes. That surprised me because I had never heard of him. The roots I had discovered in the boxes in the back of the Ford that morning were addressed to a Fernandes Nursery. The connection made sense. The whole gang was related. The report on Carlos Montalbo was depressing. The man was a walking horror show. He was too sure of himself and I was lucky that I had caught him by surprise.

I recognized the two thugs from the highway that morning with Kim Woo. Humberto Rada and his brother Miguel Rada were both cousins to Carlos Montalbo. They were not welcome in Colombia because of their various criminal activities. Made sense did it not? These punks mess up and break the law elsewhere, get run out persona non grata and they come to the good old U.S.A. where they start all over. If they had tried to enter certain other countries, like in Europe, they would have been spotted, arrested and deported immediately, but not in this country. Give me your tired, your poor, your deported criminals, your tax-dodgers, your sleeze-bags, and we will let them set up and watch them go into business doing the same low-life bunk they were doing where they came from.

The reports on North East Financial Services and the Bryn Mawr Bank and Trust Company were revealing. It wasn't clear who owned whom, but there definitely were strong financial ties between the two. Morton Bolinsky was on the board of directors of both organizations as was Carlos Montalbo, Humberto Rada, and Miguel Rada. There were others listed as officers but none of them were familiar.

It wasn't smart to buy a bank and load the board of directors with your goons when they were illegal citizens. It's not legal for a foreigner to buy into a U.S. bank and not register his ownership share with the government, let alone to take over complete control. U.S. citizenship was a necessity for Morton Bolinsky in order to own this bank, and that was probably one major reason why he faked a New York City birth certificate. As John Chusak said, "A person could get himself killed with this information." I called Jack from the bedroom and showed him the reports.

"North East Financial Services is a loan company, but Morton Bolinsky is using it for a front, as a holding company to buy the Bryn Mawr Bank and Trust," Jack said. "I know the president of that bank, Joshua Manning. He's a good man. I can't imagine how he ever got hooked up with a gang like this. If Bolinsky really isn't a U.S. citizen, then this falls under the heading of a major felony."

"They're rather obvious. Names like these are very common in Colombia but they stand out like a toad at a prince convention here in the States," I said.

"Their techniques are equally obvious. Kidnapping, extortion, and murder are common ways of doing business in South America but here that stuff doesn't fly," Jack said.

"I see now why Bolinsky moved so fast to get his boys back this morning. If we ID'd them and traced them to the Bryn Mawr Bank and Trust, it would unravel the whole scheme. He couldn't afford that so he tried a risky high profile maneuver and barged into the courtroom to retrieve his goods," I said.

"That was a desperate move. He must have panicked." Jack said.

"The part that troubles me is the lack of organization. I mean, there's organization and there's a plan somewhere behind all this, but no one seems to be thinking ahead. It's too crude. They act as if everyone should just automatically do what they want and they don't seem concerned about the consequences. It's very brazen behavior, almost as if they have total protection from the law," I said.

"That's probably how they did things in Colombia," Jack said. "They're counting on everyone being frightened and intimidated. I'll bet that you're a big surprise to Mort and his group."

"That won't last long. They'll figure it out and we'll have an even harder time cracking this thing. The problem is we have to find out where they're holding Tony Furman before we make any bold moves against Bolinsky and his group."

I showed Jack how to use the hand-held VHF radio. It was set to the company frequency assigned to Furman Airways. I stepped out on Connie's balcony overlooking the New York Central Railroad tracks, now called Metro North, flushed a couple of seagulls off the railing, and tested the radio.

We were about six miles from the airport, not a long distance, and the fourth floor location would help, but with radios one never knows. However, everything worked and Billy Jean answered immediately. She said

Kim Woo was there and I told her I'd be back soon. She asked me to pick up some more coffee and sugar on the way. Some things never change. I set up a timetable with Jack to check in every hour, straight up, and not to fail. He agreed and I left him sitting on the floor talking to his prisoner. I wondered how long it would take for one of them to crack and start confessing.

I had taken precautions to make certain I wasn't followed when I left the airport earlier, so now I wasn't looking for trouble. My father's mother, dear old grandmother Lucy, always said, "Go hunting trouble and trouble will find you." Of course she was right, but many people pretend that if they ignore reality nothing will ever happen to them. She insisted, when I was born, that I would someday be a great man of letters. Her favorite writer in the classics was William Makepeace Thackeray, author of Vanity Fair, a novel exposing the hypocrisy of the English aristocracy in the bedrooms and ballrooms of nineteenth century London during the years of the Napoleonic wars. Unfortunately, I never fulfilled her dream.

Anyway, there I was driving along minding my own business when I noticed a dark blue Ford, much like the one I'd seen earlier that morning. It was parked next to a Burger Hut. The windows were tinted but the driver's side window was open and I caught a glimpse of the driver's face. It wasn't familiar. I was about a mile from the airport entrance and I watched in my rearview mirror as they pulled out and settled into a position about two hundred yards behind me. I wasn't hunting trouble and I really wasn't interested in mixing it up with these bozos.

If it was the same duo, they wouldn't be as easy to take down a second time but curiosity got the better of me and now was a good time to find out what they were up to. I had them in my rear view mirror now but after dark they would have the advantage. Besides, I was feeling mean. I'd had my fill of these goons. Who did they think they were anyway?

"I'm not hunting trouble, Grandma. I just don't like being followed," I said to the rearview mirror and I decided to take them for a little ride.

Chapter Twelve

I drove past the airport entrance and continued around the perimeter. The interesting thing about Westchester County Airport is that it's located at the eastern boundary of the county, right smack on the Connecticut border. So when I passed the airport boundary and took a right turn off onto a smaller country road, I was in the state of Connecticut. I knew the roads in the area because Jack and I had played golf at a club not far away. I crossed a stream, took a right onto a dirt road leading into a heavily wooded area, and looked for a turn off into the trees.

I checked the rear view mirror and saw that my friends were still on my tail about a hundred yards back. I wanted them to follow me but I had an alternate plan if they didn't. The alternative was just to turn around and ram into them, a very simple but effective way to meet people, but fortunately, they followed. I rounded a curve and took a sharp turn into the woods on a small trail to the right and drove as far as I could until it became too narrow. They passed the trail and went on. It was their funeral now. The road they were on was a narrow dead end.

I backed out of the trail and across the road, blocking it, and left the engine running. I got out, pulled the

Glock out of my ankle holster, walked into the woods, and waited behind a big bush. It didn't take long. They came back slowly and stopped about fifty feet from the car and waited. I stayed out of sight and waited. They waited and I waited. They blinked first. The one on the passenger side finally got out, walked up to my Caddy and looked inside. I broke cover and stepped up to the driver's side of the Ford, opened the door, pointed the Glock at the driver's head and spoke nice words in his ear.

"Freeze, yo-yo," I yelled. He froze. "Get out very slowly and tell your buddy to put his hands up and walk back here." He did and the other one came back to the car. "Put your hands on the top of the car and spread your legs."

"You're making a big mistake, mister," said the driver. He was short with dark hair, light complexion, blue jeans, gray sweatshirt, and cowboy boots. Oh boy, just what I needed, a cowboy!

"Yeah, you don't know what you're messin' with," said the other one, a tall blond with a brush cut, broad shoulders, windbreaker, sneakers, and lots of muscle.

"Don't worry, I always bury my mistakes so I never get caught," I said, pointing the gun at the two of them.

I searched them and came up with two small .38 caliber pistols and no ID. Hell, didn't anybody carry ID's anymore? I threw the guns into the woods. They were right about one thing; I'd made a mistake. I thought they were the same two goofballs, Humberto and Miguel, that I had danced with that morning but these were new kids on the block.

"So you're the ones who made the mistake, right guys? Now tell me why you're following me and make it real good," I said.

"Look," said the little one, "we don't hafta answer any questions, so put down the gun and we'll settle this real quiet like, okay?"

He looked scared. I liked it that he looked scared because he would do what I wanted. The big one didn't look scared. He was measuring me with a very critical eye and in just a few seconds he would decide if he could take me. I decided to change his mind.

"You think you are going to take me down, big guy, but you're not because I will hurt you so bad you won't ever forget it. So just relax and stand there while we sort things out, okay?" He blinked and looked surprised but his body tensed and he shifted his weight to the balls of his feet, so I put a shot through his right foot.

"Ouch, Oh God! No! Damn you!" he said, as he sat down hard, cross-legged, and held his injured foot in both hands.

"You bastard!" said the little one. "You didn't have to do that. You'll be damn sorry when our superiors get hold of you."

"Your superiors may never hear from you again. Now persuade me that I shouldn't take you two off into the woods and finish the job, and make it the most convincing speech of your soon to be very short life," I said, and I pointed the Glock directly at his head.

"No! Wait! Okay ... We're DEA agents. You're William O'Keefe, right? You're an insurance investigator, right? We're supposed to ... uhh, talk, yeah, talk to you. That's all, just talk, okay?" He was really scared. "Please, Mr. O'Keefe, geeze-amighty man! Please?" I moved closer and put the muzzle of my gun in his ear and he started blubbering.

"Show me some ID and don't make any sudden moves," I said.

"They're in the glove compartment. We don't carry them in case we have to go undercover." He moved to open the door and I noticed his pants were wet.

"Move slow and don't try anything stupid," I said, backing up.

The big guy was sitting against the rear door so I moved back where I could cover them both. The little one was scared and didn't want to die. He handed me two pouches with badges and picture ID's. They confirmed what he said. He was Peter Drurey and the big one was Jake Gibbons, of the Drug Enforcement Administration, US Department of Justice. Everything was very official looking.

"Okay, so you're DEA. Why are you tailing me? The only drug I use is an occasional shot of Tennessee Sour Mash Whisky," I said.

"We're supposed to talk to you, that's all. We thought the Furman Airways hangar would be under surveillance so we wanted to get you away someplace where we would have more privacy," he said.

"Well, you got your wish, Pete. You almost got more privacy than you bargained for. You almost got eternal privacy. Now be specific. I don't have all day," I said.

"You're interfering in a case the DEA is currently investigating. We have several years and thousands of man-hours invested in this operation and we can't afford to lose it just because you, an insurance investigator of all things, decided to play Sir Galahad and come riding in on a white charger to save some lady friend who's got herself involved in something she can't handle," he said.

"You are not being very nice, Peter. What I do with my friends is my business, and if the DEA has an ongoing investigation that is hurting someone I know, then the DEA needs to straighten out its act. Government agencies are not supposed to infringe upon the rights of individual citizens. That may be a new concept for you but we have the Bill of Rights and the Constitution to prove it," I said.

"Okay ... Okay," Peter said. "You aren't any shining example of good conduct either. This morning you had two of Morton Bolinsky's boys picked up and later they found Carlos Montalbo all busted up in the airport parking lot. This afternoon one of our technicians disappeared, so we're here to retrieve him and warn you not to interfere any further in our operation."

"Was your technician installing a video camera in the office of Furman Airways?" I asked, moving around to my left.

"I'm not at liberty to say but we need the camera and technician back. Our funds are limited and we have other jobs waiting. I'll warn you, O'Keefe, we will not tolerate having our people tortured or injured. If you don't return our technician and that camera to us in good shape, you could face up to double life in prison and a one hundred thousand dollar fine or both." He was trying to quote the law to me from memory but he wasn't doing very well. Kidnapping was a single life crime and the camera was only worth a couple of grand.

"You know something, Peter?" I pointed the gun at his crotch. "What's to keep me from putting you two in a shallow grave out there in the woods? Then I could go on about my business and no one would know the difference. They would never find you and I wouldn't tell, so what say I do it? Tell me why I shouldn't." I grabbed his belt buckle and shoved the gun in his crotch.

"No! P ... Please ... uhh ... don't do it. We're not going to hurt anybody. Really, we were just following orders," he said.

"Shut up, Pete," Gibbons said. "He's not gonna kill ya."

"How do you know, big boy?" I asked.

"I read your bio, man. You're a cool dude and you only waste bad guys like Carlos Montalbo ... Look, you were right. I was gonna try to take you out but you didn't hafta shoot my foot. Hell, I'll be outa play for weeks with this thing. Geeze! It hurts like hell. Anyway, whadaya wanna know? We'll tell ya what you wanna know so's we can get outta here and get me to a doctor. Just say what you wanna know. Ask us anything," Jake said.

"Okay," I said. "Where's Tony Furman?"

"Don't know for sure. We'll check it out and get back to you." I kicked his foot. "OUCH! That hurts!"

"Why is Morton Bolinsky trying to take over Furman Airways?"

"We didn't know nothin' about that until this afternoon when Montalbo showed up in the hospital. That's why we sent the technician to plant the camera," Jake said.

"You guys really aren't up to date, are you?" I said.

"Shit, man, sometimes we're the last to know. Like this morning when you took out those two guys. We had a hell of a time getting them outta jail," Jake said.

"You mean Humberto and Miguel are working for you?" I asked.

"Yeah, they're our snitches. You almost got 'em deported. We gave Bolinsky an anonymous tip and he got 'em out. Man, it was close," Jake said.

"Is Bolinsky your snitch too?" I asked. I could tell he was lying.

"Hell no man, he's our target." A car came down the road and a woman in her sixties got out and looked at us from behind her open car door.

"What's going on here?" she demanded.

"Polluters," I said. "I caught these men dumping trash in the woods."

"What's wrong with him?" She pointed to Jake on the ground holding his foot.

"I had to shoot him in the foot. He tried to run away," I said.

"Good! You should shoot them all, damn polluters. They mess up everything. Moved out here to get away from the trash and now the trash comes out here to dump their trash. Shoot them all, I say."

"You want to watch while I do it? I could use some help," I said.

"Rather not. I'm not squeamish. Just don't have the time. Have to take my mother to the hairdresser's.

Damn hairdressers! Have to be there on time or they won't take you. Would you mind moving your car? I have to get going," she said.

"No problem," I said.

As she drove past she yelled out her car window. "Don't leave the bodies around here, okay? We've had three dead bodies in the last year already and it's giving the neighborhood a bad name." She waved and drove off.

"Heartless witch," said Pete.

"Tough little mamma," said Jake.

"Kinda liked her, myself," I said.

Chapter Thirteen

I decided not to shoot Jake and Pete. They didn't show any gratitude when I told them, but I'm certain they were relieved. Ingrates! At least they could have said thanks or jumped for joy or cried tears of relief. Oh well, it's hard to get good DEA agents nowadays. It was late in the afternoon when I arrived back at Furman Airways with a jar of instant coffee, a bag of sugar, and some powdered donuts that I couldn't resist buying from the shelf of the variety store. I picked up a New York Times too.

"Jack called in twice," said Billie Jean. "He sounded so excited I couldn't understand him. He said you should call him on a regular phone when you can. I think he has some information."

I thanked her and went out into the hangar where the mechanics were still working on the disabled engine. Kim Woo stood by the door watching a Cessna Cardinal doing touch and go's. He wore that perpetual smile, sort of a bemused look that I'd never seen him without. He wore civilian dress, a dark green windbreaker, dark brown slacks, and black sneakers: night time dress. His Smith and Wesson .357 Magnum was slung low on his right hip, fast draw style.

"How's it going, O'Keefe? Shoot anyone lately?" he said.

"Matter of fact I have, yes, about thirty minutes ago but not to worry, he'll live. How about you? Bust any bad guys lately?" I said.

"Yeah, but the judge keeps letting them go free. I'm in the wrong business. I should be a crook. I would spend less time in the jailhouse than I do now as a deputy sheriff." The smile persisted.

"The system doesn't work. Give it a rest Kim, get with the program and do like everyone else. Make peace with yourself, make peace with the system, and don't rock the boat," I said.

"So tell me something, Mr. O'Keefe. Have you made peace with the system, yourself, or your mother-in-law lately?" he countered.

"None of the above. That's why I live alone on the dunes among the sand fleas and sea gulls. I'm too much of a rebel to make peace with the system. It's self-perpetuating. Talk about the system perpetuating itself. I ran into a couple of DEA agents this afternoon. They were like clones from the Mickey Mouse Club," I said.

I told him about the Pete and Jake show. I told him about Montalbo, Humberto, Miguel, the technician and Jack, and the sabotage of the airplanes. Then I showed him the root I took from the trunk of the brown car that morning.

"You say there were several boxes of these in the trunk of the car?" asked Kim.

"Yes, and the shipping labels were all SPD, Speedy

Parcel Delivery, addressed to Fernandes Nursery in Southold and routed Houston to Newark," I said.

"Man, you gotta be kidding! What a scheme. You have any idea what this stuff is?" Kim said.

"Some sort of root or bulb for growing flowers, I guess."

"Wrong, my friend. This is a form of peyote. It's the portion of the mushroom that grows in the ground. This is wild stuff, not cultivated, and they shipped it with SPD?" he asked, turning it over.

"Furman Airways has contracts with SPD to operate a Dallas-Houston-Newark run," I said.

"That's neat, and I'll bet no one checks any of their cargo for drugs or other contraband," said Kim. "The air terminals are covered pretty well, but a subcontractor like Furman probably picks up their cargo directly from the SPD delivery truck so the contents of the packages are never checked. Even on the other end they probably off-load directly onto a truck. Check it out with Billy Jean."

"I thought the Port Authority had tight security at all its area terminals. I checked them out for insurance purposes a couple of times. When an aircraft arrives with a cargo, the pilot reports to the Port Authority officer to pay a landing fee and make arrangements for the transfer of the cargo. The airlines don't go through this procedure because they have their own lease rights to terminal and warehouse space, so they have to deal with the security procedures in the freight terminals where there are x-ray machines and dogs."

"Furman Airways has no lease rights so they have

to deal directly with the Port Authority security guys on a flight-by-flight basis. I wouldn't be surprised if some security guard could be bribed to look the other way, or a delivery man might be paid to stop his truck before the gate to off-load some contraband goods, but eventually someone would get wise to what was going on," I said.

"They usually do," said Kim. "Someone gets greedy and tries to grab too much and the whole scheme comes tumbling down. That's how most criminals are caught. We seldom crack a case by good investigative efforts. Criminals usually get caught because they're careless or stupid. Take this peyote bulb. You would never have found it if those two goons who tailed you this morning had any brains. One of the first rules in the drug business is never to get caught with the goods in your possession. What that means is, don't do anything stupid while you're carrying," Kim said.

"I'm not going to underestimate this gang," I said. "They may not be the smartest bunch but they're dangerous. I'm going to stay on their tail until I've got them beaten and then I'll see to it they go back where they came from. We don't need the Morton Bolinskys of this world. When I finish with him, he'll wish he never stepped foot in this country. Let him go back to the sewer he was born in."

"Do you feel that way about all foreigners?" asked Kim.

"Not at all. I respect anyone who has the courage to leave his home and move to a strange new country. This nation was built on the differences between its people and upon the premise that everyone should have equal opportunity. Everyone should have the right to achieve a decent and comfortable living without being subjected to intimidation, blackmail, and extortion by a privileged class of thugs who buy protection with bribery, murder, and shyster lawyers," I said.

"You're full of surprises, O'Keefe," said Kim, a smile broadening across his face. "I thought you were just a cynical white American redneck who carries a gun and chases dumb blonds to keep his ego pumped up. Instead, I find you're a true patriot who believes in fair play and equality for all."

"My secret is out. Now I can't play the tough guy act any more. Everyone will laugh when I say 'stick 'em up'. I'll have to give up blonds and settle for smart brunettes instead," I said.

"Gee whiz, Bill. I didn't mean to ruin your sex life. Tell you what, if you want me to keep quiet just pay me a million dollars and I'll keep it to myself," said Woo.

"That's blackmail, you two faced son of Chan," I said.

"Does that mean I have to go back where I came from?" asked Kim. "My parents are from Korea. I'm a full-blooded American, born right here in White Plains, so I can stay here if I want to and you can't make me leave."

"Figures. I guess I'll have to pay you the million dollars after all."

"Very smart decision, mick."

It was always fun to have a philosophical discussion with Kim. He was intelligent and there wasn't a subject he couldn't discuss and if there was, he'd go look it up, come back, and give you the answer. He was a walking encyclopedia and I always enjoyed testing him when we got together. He was an intelligence officer in the Air Force and had done time in some of the hot spots of the world as a military advisor. He had the qualifications for the job and with him there I could rest easy and go on with my investigations. I filled him in on my plans and went to the office to talk to Billy Jean.

"I have a business to operate," she said. "I have to keep these aircraft flying or I'll lose those contracts, and they're the bread and butter that keep us alive. I've cancelled the ground school classes and the student flight appointments for now. I told everyone that we're short handed and we'll be back up and running in a week or so. I just wish you would find Tony and bring him back so we could put this thing behind us."

"I can go looking for Tony and I might even find him and with luck bring him back, but that won't stop the criminals from pursuing Furman Airways and harassing you and your family. I need to gather intelligence on these people so I can make one decisive move against them, get Tony back, and put a permanent end to Morton Bolinsky and his plans," I said.

"When will that be? Billy Jean asked.

"There's another angle to this that you need to understand. We're assuming that Bolinsky is the kidnapper. We don't know that for certain even if it fits. If he is, he'll keep Tony alive only so long as there is some benefit in doing so. If I move on Bolinsky and I fail, he may not keep Tony alive. I can't risk that. Timing is everything.

My plan is to keep them coming to us until we're ready to move. Then we wipe them out," I said.

"You sound pretty confident but so far the only thing you've done is kick some punk in the head when he wasn't looking, and chase another one out the back door," she said.

"You're being unkind, babe. What's the problem? What's going on?" I asked.

"It's not you, Bill. Oh, darn it! I had another phone call. This time they let me talk to Tony. It was awful. He ... they said that he could come back if we got rid of you and turned the business over to them. They're willing to give us a million dollars in cash and they won't hurt anyone. Do you know how much a million dollars tax-free is? We've never seen that sort of money, Tony or me. Bill, it's a way out." She started crying.

"I don't think so but it's your choice. They'll do anything to get their way and that includes murder. I doubt you'll ever see the million even if you agree to what they want," I said.

"But they said ..." she stopped and sobbed.

"They said what you wanted to hear! Good grief, Billy Jean. If someone came through that door right now and said he was a pilot and wanted to fly for you, what's the first thing you'd do?" I said.

"What's this got to do with anything?" she said.

"Just answer the question, lady. He says he's a pilot. What do you do?" I asked.

"I ask to see his pilot certification, medical, flight log, and a resume´ of where he's worked," she said.

"Right, and if you found out he crashed every aircraft

he ever flew, that he was wanted for every major felony in ten different countries, and he couldn't give you one single decent supportive reference, what would you do then?" I asked.

"That's ridiculous. I'd never hire such a person," said Billy Jean.

"Then why do you even consider doing business with these kidnappers? They're bozos. They have a reputation for not doing what they promise. They rape, kidnap, murder, extort, intimidate, and lie, so what makes you think they'll live up to their word, give you a million dollars, and let you walk away with no cuts or bruises? Get real, Billy Jean! They don't leave witnesses and they don't pay for what they can take for nothing. There are no neat, clear rules and regulations for what Bolinsky is doing to you. Anything goes in this game and the winner is the one still standing when the smoke clears."

"You make it sound like a Wild West show. This is the twenty-first century and we're living in New York. We have laws. What's the government doing about these druggie people, anyway?" she said.

So I told her. I showed her the profiles I received from John Chusak in Chicago. I explained about the DEA and the two clones, Jake and Pete, and how I caught them tailing me that afternoon, and how it seems they had some real big investigation going on that was more important than what was happening to her and Furman Airways.

I told her about Morton Bolinsky and how his two goons, Humberto and Miguel, were supposed to be DEA informants working for Pete and Jake, but no one seemed to know anything about Tony Furman being kidnapped. This made me suspect three possibilities: Pete and Jake were dirty, Humberto and Miguel really were not playing it straight with the DEA, or we were on the wrong track and Morton Bolinsky was the Pope.

"So you see, there really aren't that many options," I said.

"But if the DEA is messing things up, can't we call the FBI or somebody else to go straighten them out?" she asked.

"When one government agency is involved in an investigation, no other government agency will cross into the other's jurisdiction, so don't count on help from the government because they can't help themselves. Actually, it's worse than that. If the DEA is doing an investigation, it tells the FBI to stay away, so the FBI stands back and makes no moves even if they should. That amounts to protection for the ones involved in the investigation. They have to do something pretty bad to break that barrier," I said.

"So, you're telling me there's no way out. What am I supposed to do?" She asked, as she came to me and started crying.

We had this conversation before but she needed reassurance, especially after hearing her husband's voice. That would do a number on anyone but she was especially vulnerable with the pressures of running Furman Airways. The bad guys were getting smarter. They were going for the heartstrings.

"Like I told you this morning, lady, you'll just have to trust me. I have some troops on the job for protection. I found someone to finance your business and I've identified some of the key bad guys. I caught four dudes tailing me, two intruders here in the hangar, one planting a bomb in your instrument trainer and one planting a surveillance camera in your office, and I nailed one of the worst assassins in the Western hemisphere. Believe what you want but I've been on the job less than twelve hours and I've done all that," I said.

"I know, I know, but they said they will give Tony back if we just walk away. I don't care about the million dollars. You're right, maybe they're playing games, but what can I do?" She stopped crying and I let go of her.

"Trust me. Remember, they also stipulated that you have to get rid of me. That means they're worried. The thing that puzzles me is why go to all this trouble just to smuggle some psycho-mushrooms out of Texas into New York City? They don't go outside the U.S. borders. If it was cocaine or heroin they were bringing in, and they needed the aircraft to fly over the border, that would seem logical. Otherwise, why go to all this trouble?" I said.

"Maybe it isn't drugs they're smuggling," said Billy Jean.

"That makes sense, except what else is worth all the time and expense? The government's efforts to shut down drug smuggling have been very effective in some areas. Many traditional conduits used by the drug cartels have been shut down, so it stands to reason they would be looking for alternative routes. Owning a small air taxi operation like this would solve many of their smuggling problems."

"I just don't know. I suppose we'll find out before long, but I have a flight to Miami due to leave in an hour and the SPD and mail trucks will arrive any minute." She stood, gave me a peck on the cheek, and walked out of the office, a troubled woman.

I went into the hangar where Mickey had the damaged plane apart and one man was replacing rivets in the engine supports.

"We have it cleaned out," said Mickey, "and we crated up the damaged engine for return to Reworks in Wichita when Linda does her Dallas-Houston trip tomorrow night. By the time she returns on Saturday, we should be ready for the new engine. We'll have this aircraft back on line by Sunday afternoon at the latest, barring any more catastrophes." He shook his head in disgust.

"You look tired, Mickey. When do you rest?" I asked.

"I'll catch some sleep on a cot up above the office. There are three cots up there. We use them when we don't have time to go home. You can do the same, Bill. Nobody minds," he said.

"Thanks, I may just do that," I said.

The mail truck had arrived and Billy Jean was loading mail sacks with Jimmy Linn's help into an old Aero Commander 590.

"We'll have a problem if the SPD load is bigger than normal," said Billy Jean. "This aircraft doesn't have the payload of the Beech-99. We may have to activate the C-123 and hire more pilots."

"That doesn't sound so bad," I said, grabbing a bag and carrying it to the door of the airplane.

"We mothballed the C-123 because it was too slow

and expensive to operate. Those big radial engines suck up gas like an alcoholic in a brewery. We made money if we had a full load, but most of the time we ran partial loads and the FAA regs required us to staff two pilots and provide overnights and per diem pay. We can fly these smaller aircraft with a single pilot, and as long as it's one of the family, we cut out the overnight and the extra flight pay," she said.

"Sounds complicated," I said.

"It's a complicated business, and it's heavy work too," she said.

After we finished loading the last mail sack, I wandered back to the hangar. I was behind another airplane parked on the tarmac when a small panel truck came around the corner of the hangar and stopped next to the Aero Commander where the mail truck was just departing. The name on the side of the truck was there in bold letters and easily read even in the growing darkness: Speedy Parcel Delivery. I was turning to walk back in order to help when the driver of the truck opened his door and stepped out.

'You could have knocked me over with a feather', as the saying goes. There, standing at the back of the SPD truck, handing packages and crates to Billy Jean and Jimmy Linn for loading onto the Aero Commander, was our old friend from that afternoon in the woods, DEA agent Pete Drurey. I backed into the shadows and played chameleon as I watched the government's undercover agent deliver the goods.

I had the impulse to just stroll out there and confront the little jerk, but my intuition told me to play it cool.

Something was very wrong, but I needed time to find out what it was before I jumped in and muddied up the waters. I stood there, transfixed by the irony of it all. There was a movement behind me and I turned to find Kim standing there. He moved like a cat.

"What's going on, O'Keefe? You look like the Great White Hunter stalking an elephant," he said.

"You're right about that, except it's not an elephant," I said. "It's a hyena!"

Chapter Fourteen

WE watched the loading of the aircraft, and no sooner was the last package on board and the cargo door closed then Pete Drurey was on the move, clipboard in hand, into the cab of the truck and gone back the way he came, as if he were really an SPD delivery man with a schedule to complete. He didn't even look around the flight line. He just got his bill of lading signed and off he went. Jimmy Linn was starting the engines and taxiing for the runway while Billy Jean walked back toward the hangar. She didn't see Kim or me in the shadows.

"Wonder what that was all about?" said Kim. "If this fellow is with the DEA and he has inside men working for him in Morton Bolinsky's organization, then why is he driving a delivery truck?"

"Maybe he's moonlighting," I said. "What bothers me is that he didn't even look around him. He wasn't the least bit curious about what was going on in the general area of Furman Airways. All he did was concentrate on getting those crates on board the aircraft."

"Yeah, I'd like to know what's in those boxes. Did you notice anything strange about them?" Kim asked.

"Yes, about half of them were the same, rectangular

wooden crates about two feet square. Must have been all from the same company," I said.

"Yes, and they looked heavy," said Kim. "Why ship something that heavy by airfreight? It must get expensive."

"Let's check with Billy Jean." We found her sitting at her desk.

"Where did you disappear to when the heavy stuff came in, O'Keefe? We could have used your muscles," she said.

"I got sidetracked. Is that the same driver you have every day or do they change?" I asked.

"They used to change a lot, but for the past month this fellow has made the deliveries. He's the fastest one we've had," she said.

"Do you have a list of the boxes shipped?" asked Kim.

"No, Jimmy Linn has that on the aircraft. He'll check the crates as they're off-loaded in Miami. We run such a tight schedule, we don't take time to copy the list. I suppose we should but it's one more thing to do and I'm exhausted," she said.

"What was in those wooden crates? There must have been about twenty of them," I said.

"Twenty-two to be exact. They were marked 'Ball Bearings', from a company in Connecticut. If you're really interested, you can check the paperwork tomorrow when Jimmy Linn comes back. I have lists in the files from the same company from previous flights." She opened a file cabinet drawer and handed Kim a folder marked "SPD-Current Month". We looked through the shipping lists and saw the same company listed on almost every flight, Hi-Tec Ball Bearings, of Bridgeport, Connecticut.

"Do they ship those crates on almost every flight to Miami or Dallas?" I asked.

"Yes, every flight. Actually, they go to Houston, not Dallas. I never paid much attention. We get paid by the pound and those crates are heavy. They're good money-makers and I don't want to lose them," she said.

"How long have you been handling them?" Kim asked.

"It's only been the past month," she said.

"Since that new driver has been on the job?" I suggested.

"Yes, you're right. Isn't that a coincidence?" she said.

"Not really," I said, flipping through the pages.

"Not at all. Must be a hell of a demand for ball bearings in Miami and Houston," Kim said.

"Yes, things are really on a roll down south," I said.

"What are you two talking about?" she asked.

"Not sure, but I'd like to see what's in those crates when the next shipment arrives," I said.

"That'll be tomorrow night when Linda takes her trip to Dallas and Houston. It may be difficult for you to open one before the aircraft departs, because the SPD driver insists on the door of the airplane being closed before he leaves. Sort of odd but he says he likes to see his cargo take off. It gives him a feeling of satisfaction."

"I'll bet it does. Maybe I can stow away and get off just before Linda takes off," I said.

"Why don't you just go with her on the trip," Billy Jean suggested. "She could use the company and some extra help with loading the new engine in Wichita."

I objected, saying I couldn't afford to be away that long, but both Kim and Billy Jean insisted they could handle things in my absence. I had no intention of taking them up on it, however, and I take no responsibility for the consequences. It was not my idea. I didn't want to do it and it's not my fault, but ... well, you'll see what I mean.

"Has Jack called in since I got back?" I asked, changing the subject.

"Not that I know of," said Billy Jean. Kim agreed.

I picked up the microphone on the company radio unit and called him but got no answer. I tried several more times with no results. Then Billy Jean tried. I walked to the pay phones at the corner of the main terminal and called Connie's apartment. No answer. I told Kim to stay put and raced to Connie's apartment driving over the speed limit all the way. I found the door open when I arrived, so I pulled the Glock and checked the place out.

Jack was in the bathroom, stark naked, lying on his back, his feet up in the air tied to the shower curtain pole. His head was under the shower, cold water spraying on his body. His hands were tied behind him and there was a gag in his mouth: water torture, and a very professional job. When he saw me, he started struggling against the ropes and making funny growling noises. I turned the water off, cut the ropes loose with my grandfather's pocket knife, stood him up, and helped him out of the bathtub. He was blue and his teeth were chattering from the coldwater treatment.

""Ba-Bas-Bas-tard!" he chattered as I toweled him off and got him dressed. It took hot tea and blankets with a quick rubdown before he could talk again. Seems the technician/prisoner pulled a fast one. He feigned having to go to the toilet, number two, needed his hands free, and Jack fell for it and even let the man close the bathroom door for privacy.

"He came out of the bathroom and roped me like I was a rodeo calf before I could blink. Damn it, Bill, you told me not to untie him and you were right. He called someone and they came here. They made me strip and tied me up in the bathtub and turned on the cold shower. They flipped the drain lever so the tub would fill up with water and drown me. I was able to bump the lever back up so the drain worked but then it got so cold I couldn't move. I would have died of hypothermia if you hadn't come when you did," he said.

"Describe the people who came and tied you up," I said.

"They were both big. One was dark skinned and spoke only Spanish. I couldn't make out most of it. He spoke too fast. The other one was American and he was on crutches. His right foot was all bandaged up and he seemed to be in charge. One of them called him Jake. I think it was his idea to tie me up. He spoke fluent Spanish. I think I heard your name and they weren't too happy with you," he said.

"That was Jake Gibbons, claims to be a DEA agent but I think he's dirty. I shot him in the foot this afternoon when I left here. It's a long story but I'm just glad you're all right. Were you able to get anything out of your prisoner before he got loose?"

"He said that we were going to regret what we were doing. He said it wouldn't do us any good to call the FBI because they had protection and they could do whatever they wanted. He asked me where you went and I told him you had gone to find a priest for him to talk to. That's when I called you. I thought he was ready to talk. I think he was just sizing me up until he thought of a way to get loose. Man, do I feel like a fool," Jack said.

"You were up against a professional who's been trained to survive capture and interrogation. These aren't your ordinary drug cartel goons. If I run into him or his friends again, I won't be so nice, especially with our friend Jake," I said.

I showed Jack the profiles from John Chusak and he identified Humberto Rada as one of the two who tied him up. Since Jake Gibbons was there too and seemed to be giving the orders, it meant he was dirty. No agent, even an undercover DEA agent, would participate in such an atrocity. Jack was starting to feel better but I didn't dare leave him at Connie's apartment. The goon squad might return. I called in on the radio to let the troops at Furman Airways know we were all right. I faxed a message to John Chusak requesting information on Peter Drurey and Jake Gibbons, alleged DEA agents. Then I called Connie in Wilson, Iowa.

"Bill, I'm so glad you called. Dad is better and the doctors say he'll be out of danger soon if he continues to improve through the night. It's such a relief to everyone," she said. "They said he might not make a full recovery, however, but he'll live."

We talked for a while and I told her briefly about Morton Bolinsky's attempt to take over Furman Airways. I left out the gory details and concentrated on how brilliant I was at solving the case. We said the goofy stuff that couples say when they miss each other and I promised to call her tomorrow. I looked around the apartment and experienced an incredible sense of loneliness. Connie was an unusual lady in every way. She had grown up on a farm in Iowa and then she broke out of that and became a top executive in an international corporation where competition was like breathing: it never went way. The thing I admired most about her was that she was a person of integrity, and she kept that even as she worked in the corporate world in spite of all the muck-raking bottom feeders with all their intrigue and back-stabbing. She was as steady as they came and I missed her.

Our modern lives are so fast-paced and hectic that our bodies are in one place while our brains are in another. Just last night I was in the arms of my love, and since then, I had done everything but commit murder, and that could happen before morning at the rate things were going. I had to get some sleep and keep my mind on what I was doing. I should never have left Jack alone. He was a great banker, an excellent pilot and an all around good guy, but he was not an interrogator. Our prisoner was smart enough to wait until I was gone to make his move, and very effective he was too.

Jack was asleep on Connie's bed. He wasn't good at handling trauma and that's what it was when he realized he might die in that bathtub. I thought of leaving him there but dismissed the idea, so I called Kim on the radio and told him I'd be staying at Connie's for awhile. I set the clock radio for midnight, laid down on the couch, and promptly dozed off into a land of sleep that was almost more painful than being awake. I had nightmares peopled by Colombian drug lords who all looked like Carlos Montalbo carrying machetes. I was naked and he was chasing me through the jungle with ice-cold rain falling. I woke up in a cold sweat, sorry I had even gone to sleep.

I put on the kettle, took a quick hot shower and changed into clean clothes. Jack was awake by then so we had our coffee and headed back to the airport. I stopped at a Burger Hut and picked up a dozen burger bangers with cheese, three brown cows (chocolate milk) three white cows (white milk), six Isaac Newtons (hot apple pies) and six orders of couch potatoes (French fries). Jack said something about junk food but I noticed he ate his share when we got to Furman Airways.

"Man, you really know how to take care of the troops," said Kim between bites. "You're all right, O'Keefe. This is real class gourmet treats," he said as he took a long draw on his brown cow.

"An army travels on its belly," I said.
"Who said that?" asked Jack, munching his burger.
"Caesar, I think."
"No, it was George Patton."
"You're both wrong, it was Douglas MacArthur."
"No, no. He said, 'I will return'."
"Exactly," I said, as I inhaled another Isaac Newton.

Chapter Fifteen

It was after one o'clock in the morning. The airport was quiet and its white runway lights shown dimly in the evening mist as it settled over the surface of the runway. The blue glow of the taxiway lights in the foreground offered a soft contrast to the darkness beyond as I scanned the area. Our job was to protect Furman Airways, its assets and employees, but I had to go further and find out where these people were and what they were doing. Then I could go looking for Tony Furman and put a stop to Morton Bolinsky and his evil plans.

"One thing at a time, O'Keefe," I told myself.

If there was an attempt to break in tonight or damage anything, we had to be ready. I couldn't afford to get all foggy-bottomed about what might happen tomorrow. I had my Glock in the left ankle holster and a Special Forces knife that I had borrowed from Kim on my right ankle. In addition, I was carrying the .44 Magnum in a shoulder holster slung left with extra ammo. I took a cue from Kim and wore a dark outfit: pants, shirt, windbreaker, and sneakers.

I checked the side of the hangar facing the road and made a mental note of the parked cars and their positions. I parked my Caddy in front of the hangar next to a Piper Cherokee, put the ignition keys in my pocket and left the door unlocked. I told Kim I'd take the watch until dawn.

I checked both sides of the hangar area and the parked aircraft but found nothing out of the ordinary. The sodium lights atop the hangar cast eerie shadows on the surrounding scene, reminding me of the flares we used in Vietnam to light the landscape at night. I settled down and waited, sitting on the tire of an aircraft, using the landing strut as a backrest. I thought this was a good way to watch things and I would fall off the tire and wake up if I fell asleep. It was a good plan and it worked.

I woke up lying on the asphalt under the wing of the aircraft. It was after five o'clock in the morning. I didn't remember falling asleep and for a moment I wasn't sure where I was, so I just lay there and took inventory.

Captain Matthew Thornton of Midland, Texas, my CO in Vietnam, always said, "If you wake up suddenly and you're not sure what's happening, don't just jump up and start looking around for some action because action will probably find you first."

I scanned the area but saw nothing out of place around the hangar. I shifted and looked around the tire, out in the direction of the runway. It was still early, the mist on the ground was lifting and the runway lights were glowing brightly in the darkness. I was about to sit up when I noticed that one of the white runway lights to the right blinked. Then another one did the same and a blue light to the left blinked.

I was under an airplane, lying prone on the asphalt about a hundred yards from the main north-south runway at five o'clock in the morning, and there were lights blinking at me and they weren't supposed to do that. I thought at first it might be sea gulls on the runway. They like to gather there for some reason during the day so maybe they were there now. I shifted back and squinted into the darkness. As my eyesight adjusted to the darkness, I saw three, maybe four forms coming across the runway and onto the grass strip separating the runway from the main parallel taxiway, and they weren't sea gulls. I thought at first they might be maintenance workers but they would have had lights and they wouldn't be spread out in an advancing line, dressed in dark outfits like these were.

I pulled the Glock out of my ankle holster, removed the two spare clips, and stuffed them in my jacket pocket. I had to be careful because there are all sorts of people wandering about airports and I didn't want to make a mistake and blow away the airport's light bulb changing crew or the runway sweeper's union. My reputation for being trigger-happy was already well established. I watched from my semi-fetal position as the forms advanced past the taxiway to the edge of the tarmac, where the dim glow of the hangar lights cut into the darkness.

They stopped there about seventy-five yards away, each crouched into a kneeling position, weapons in hand reflecting the light. There were five of them and they weren't changing light bulbs or sweeping the runway. I would probably not hit anything if I started shooting now but it would alert my troops and we would scare them off. I could wait and take out a couple hoping the rest wouldn't make it to the hangar, but what if they got behind me?

They came all at once, spread out about ten feet apart in a line abreast. I waited until they were about fifty feet away and took out the two in the middle right. The one on the end, to my right, cut loose with automatic fire but he was running and his aim wasn't good. I rolled to my right and came up firing. He tripped and went flat on his face. The other two were firing but I didn't wait around. I charged for the darkness to the right, firing on the run as I headed toward the runway and away from the airplanes and hangar.

As I ran, I heard the report of a much larger weapon from the hangar area. I made it across the taxiway and literally dove onto the grass strip beyond. I rolled and lay prone, taking aim at the two attackers who were still left. They were lying down firing at the hangar. One of the wounded gunmen was still in action and he was shooting my way. The access door of the hangar was partially open and behind it I could see Kim firing his .357 Magnum. We messed up their Plan A and they were now trapped in the open with no Plan B.

I was on my third clip but I was not within effective range, so I switched to my .44 Magnum. Just then I heard the roar of an engine and turned to see a pickup truck racing down the taxiway, its lights out. There was a shooter in the back spraying the whole area with bullets. It pulled up beside the two remaining gunmen, who proceeded to climb in. They tried to help the wounded man aboard but he couldn't move fast enough so they left him. Both Kim and I poured our last shots into the pickup, doing as much damage as possible as it cut around the corner of the hangar and disappeared. I waited as Kim came out from behind the metal hangar access door and advanced slowly on the two bodies on the asphalt. When he was next to them, I hailed him but I didn't jump up and go running in. I waited for him to acknowledge and wave me in before I stood up and walked slowly into the lighted area with my hands at my side.

"You all right?" Kim asked.

"Yeah, I'm fine, just a bit pumped," I answered.

"Are you sure?" he said, looking at me.

"Of course. I didn't give them a chance to get a clear shot."

I kicked the gun away from one of the bodies and noticed there was a lot of blood on the asphalt. Billy Jean and Jack were coming toward us and they were walking funny, like they were drunk. Kim was standing next to me, holding on to my arm like he was afraid he might fall over, so I offered to carry him to the hangar.

"Are you okay?" Billy Jean asked, looking frightened.

"Sure, everything's fine. We stopped them cold. Got all of em."

"He's losing it," said Jack. "He's covered with blood."

"I think he stopped a couple," said Kim.

"You're all crazy," I said. Then somebody turned out the lights.

Chapter Sixteen

I wasn't out for long. When I came to I was in the hangar on a cot. People were all around me and there was a buzzing sound like someone was operating one of those small, hand held orbital sanders. It was loud, and when I turned to see where it was the pain in my head became intolerable.

"Easy does it, pal." A man in a white outfit was bending over me. "You've been shot, buddy, and you gotta stay quiet while we get the bleeding stopped," he yelled.

I did what he said because everything hurt, especially my head. Billy Jean was leaning over me saying something but the sound of the orbital sander was louder than before, so I couldn't hear her. She was crying and a tear fell on my face. I tried to tell her it was all right but my jaw wouldn't move. I couldn't feel it so I reached up to see if it was there and found a big gauze bandage where my jaw was supposed to be.

"Take it easy, pal!" The man in white was yelling in my face again. He had onion breath and bad bedside manners.

I said the hell with it and closed my eyes. When I opened them again I was someplace else. A voice was saying, "Take it easy, Mr. O'Keefe. You'll be just fine.

You're in a hospital. We're going to patch you up. We've stopped the bleeding and you're going to be okay."

I tried to say something but it didn't make sense. My head hurt like hell.

"What did he say, Nurse?"

"Sounded like wire, Doctor. He said, 'Did they get over the wire'?"

"He's delirious, not making sense. Wow, look at the scars. What made those?"

"Those are bullet holes, Nurse. This fellow must lead a very interesting life."

"He said something else, Doctor. Sounded like King Kong on the wire. He's really out of it. He thinks he's at the movies. Shall I sedate him more?"

"No, he's someplace else. He's not delirious. He thinks he's in Vietnam and the Viet Cong are attacking, trying to breach the wire. Tell him everything ... never mind, I'll tell him. O'Keefe! Everything is okay, man. You stopped them all, buddy. None of them made it past the wire."

"What's he doing? He's holding up his hand."

"Thumbs up, Nurse. He's giving us the thumbs up ... He's right too. Considering the body count tonight, this guy must have been something else out there. He literally walked through fire. All right, he's done. Bring in the next one."

The following hours were spent between restless sleep and painful consciousness. The doctor came in and I realized I wasn't alone. Billy Jean was curled up in a chair next to my bed.

"Can you hear me, Mr. O'Keefe?" The doctor was leaning over me. His nametag read 'Dr. Mancuso.'

"Of course, Doc. You don't have to yell." My head hurt but my jaw moved. The bandage was gone.

"That's good. Do you remember what happened?" he asked.

"Yeah, I fell asleep ... and ..."

"No, no, no, Mr. O'Keefe, you didn't fall asleep. You were shot in the leg and head. You were in a gun battle," he said.

"I know that, doctor. There were five of them. I took three and Kim Woo went after the other two."

"There were only three brought in," said Doctor Mancuso. "One was dead, the other two were badly wounded. They're in the critical care unit downstairs. One had chest wounds. We took five nine-millimeter slugs out of him. The other one was hit by a single .357 Magnum slug in the stomach. Tore him up badly."

"Two escaped," said Billy Jean. "They left a trail of blood but they got away."

I tried sitting up and found it painful but possible. The doctor helped me. I was in a hospital room with beige curtains. The sun slanted through the windows at an angle that told me it was either late afternoon or early morning. My head hurt but not like before.

"What time is it?" I asked. "What day is it?"

"It's 3:00 in the afternoon, Friday. Why?" asked Billy Jean.

"The bank, we have to get to the bank before it closes so we can make the mortgage payment. They'll foreclose if we don't pay them ..."

"Don't worry, Jack is taking care of it right now. He'll be in later, as soon as he's finished. "Kim Woo is watching the hangar and Mickey is still working on the King Air," Billy Jean said.

"What about Linda? Is she taking the trip to Dallas tonight? She shouldn't go alone. It's not safe."

"Don't worry about it, Mr. O'Keefe," said the doctor. "You're not going anywhere. Your wounds aren't critical but you have to rest. You have a puncture wound in your left thigh that required some stitching. It bled a lot. Your head wound is superficial but it also bled a lot. You are very lucky. From what I hear, there was a regular war out there."

"I've got to get out of here," I said, trying to get out of bed.

"Oh, no, you can't leave quite yet. We'll have to see how you heal first. Maybe three or four days from now we'll talk about you leaving," said the doctor.

"I can't stay here three more hours, Doc. I have work to do and people depending on me," I said, struggling with the blanket.

"I can't let you go anywhere right now, Mr. O'Keefe. I can't take the responsibility for what might happen," said Dr. Mancuso.

"I'll take responsibility, Doctor. Just give me some painkillers and show me where the bandage is and I'll be out of your hair. I've got nothing against hospitals but there are some very bad people out there trying to hurt my friends. They need a disreputable coyote like me to protect them, so please, just give me some pills and let me get back to doing what I do best."

"And exactly what do you do best?" asked Dr. Mancuso.

"I mess up the bad guys before they hurt innocent people."

"Sort of a King Arthur or a John Wayne?" he asked, smiling.

"I'm not in their class, Doc, more like Little Orphan Annie."

"You think you're pretty tough, don't you, Mr. O'Keefe. You lost a lot of blood and you need rest and medical care," he said.

"That's fine with me, Doc, as long as I can do it from a strategic position with my back to a wall and a gun in my hand. I'll rest all you want but not here," I said, looking around for my clothes.

"I'll see to it he gets some rest," said Billy Jean. "He won't relax as long as he's in here. He might as well come back where we can watch him and he'll feel like he's doing something important."

"I see," said Doctor Mancuso, looking at my chart. "Well, okay. I'll let you go but by what's holy, I'll not take responsibility for what happens to you. You tough guys really tick me off. We get your type in here every day of the week. We've got one upstairs under police guard right now. He came in yesterday with a smashed chest and cerebral hemorrhage. They found him in the parking lot of the airport. I don't suppose you know anything about that do you, Mr. O'Keefe?"

"Was he a tall fellow, dark hair, answered to the name of Carlos, and carried a .357 Magnum?" I asked.

"Yes, so you know him," Dr. Mancuso said, smiling.

"No, Doc, never heard of him but he's got some friends and they aren't nice, and that's why I have to get back and look after the chickens, as they say."

"You are some piece of work, O'Keefe. Sign your name right here," said Dr. Mancuso, handing me his clipboard.

They wheeled me out of the hospital an hour later. Doctor Mancuso personally pushed me out the door in a wheelchair, clucking like a mother hen the whole way. Jack Sullivan met us in my Caddy and drove us back to Furman Airways. He briefed me about the day's activities on the way.

"I nailed Josh Manning at the Bryn Mawr Bank and Trust first thing this morning," said Jack. "He tried playing dumb but we've known each other too long. I threatened to turn him in to the banking commissioner and he cracked. They threatened his family. Morton Bolinsky bought a controlling share in the Bryn Mawr bank early last summer. Josh doesn't know how it happened but his major stockholders just dropped out. Bolinsky showed up with his goons and took control. Never a question of foreign ownership because Bolinsky is supposed to be a U.S. citizen. I scared him good when I told him who Carlos Montalbo and the others were, and how Bolinsky is tied into the drug business."

"So, did you get Furman Airways straightened out with him?"

"Better than you can imagine. I called my bank and had them do a buyout on the Furman Airways contract. I own it now and nobody can foreclose unless I say so," said Jack, a banker's look of satisfaction on his face.

"Josh Manning was so scared he had to go to the men's room three times while I was there. He was calling his lawyer on one line and the FBI on the other when I left. What do you think? Will Morton Bolinsky be a busy man after this?" he said.

"More than you can imagine," I answered, trying to find a comfortable position for my leg.

It was late afternoon when we arrived at the airport. I set myself down in a chaisse lounge just inside the office where I could look out the window. The painkillers were working and I was feeling pretty chipper. Billy Jean brought in some Chinese food and we chowed down big time.

"Looks like you got your appetite back," said Kim. "I didn't know getting shot did that to a man." He scoffed an egg roll and dipped it in duck sauce. "You know, I been in a lot of battles but I never ate so good. You guys really know how to put on a war."

"I haven't eaten since last night, Kim, and I've had a lot of exercise since then," I said.

"You're going to get some more. The local cops aren't happy. They want to talk to you. My boss is on my case too. We're allowed to moonlight but stepping into gun battles like the one this morning is frowned upon. I'll get by but my boss, the sheriff, is taking some heat and he'll pass some of it down to me," Kim said.

"Sorry about that. Unfortunately, it's one of the prices you pay for being part of the system. Morton Bolinsky should be getting the heat. He should be accountable," I said.

"True. We're accountable, but those guys aren't.

We don't know who they are. They had Latino features but no identification and there are no records on them anywhere," said Kim.

"Figures. Illegals," I said.

"Yes, the police will have to go to Colombia and even then they may not identify anyone," Kim said.

We talked and ate and talked some more and it looked as if that was it for the day. I was beginning to feel pretty mellow, and even with the mild headache and a low level of discomfort in my left leg, I drifted off into a deep sleep. The pharmaceutical solution always works best.

Chapter Seventeen

I woke up to find a man shaking me by the shoulder. He was a cop. I could tell because he was big with short spiked blond hair, in his mid thirties, slightly overweight, with "Jerk" written all over him. You know, the sort of fellow who's used to intimidating his way through life. He had a gun under his left arm and a badge on his belt.

Kim Woo stood up. "Hi Bobby. This is Chief of Detectives Bobby Ragan from the local police," he said to me.

I didn't stand and I didn't shake his hand. Billy Jean said 'Hi'. Jack Sullivan, always the gentleman, shook his hand but then bankers shake everyone's hand. Mickey excused himself and Linda said she had to prepare for her flight to Dallas.

"You O'Keefe?" Ragan demanded, aggressively pointing his finger at me.

I just looked at him. Some people never get it. They go through life shoving and pushing, throwing their weight around, unaware of the consequences. I could see the reddish blush growing up his neck and around his ears: hypertension.

"I asked you a question, buster." He advanced at my chair like a charging bull.

I still didn't answer him. Instead, I fished another pork strip out of a box and dipped it in duck sauce.

"You wanna come downtown and spend some time in a cell, pal? You got a choice and you better make it right now. You understand me?" he said, standing over me in a threatening way his finger punching me in the chest.

"Tell me something, Detective," I said in a nice, easy voice.

"What?" he sneered.

"Have you had your feeding yet today or are you just naturally rude?" I offered him the pork strip and he slapped it away.

"Hold it, Bobby!" said Kim, stepping in between us. "Just take it easy." He pulled Ragan back.

"I'll take it easy, Woo, when this bum does what he's told. I got one man dead and two critically wounded men in the hospital. I got another one we found in the parking lot out there and that looks a lot like his dirty work. I got all I need to put this O'Keefe away for assault with intent to commit murder and murder one, so don't mess with me, buster," he growled.

"Why don't you let me help out here?" asked Kim. "Bill, Detective Ragan just wants to ask a few questions. He's upset because of the body count the past few days. Can't say I blame him. We're not used to this sort of Wild West show and Detective Ragan just needs some answers."

Kim was playing the good-guy, bad-guy routine. I was familiar with it so I played along.

"I'll be glad to tell you whatever you need to know,

but put meathead there," I pointed to Ragan, "back on his chain. I don't think he's had his rabies shots."

Ragan tried to push Kim aside to get at me but Kim blocked him. "Take it easy, Bobby. O'Keefe just likes pulling your chain."

"Why's he doin' it?" demanded Ragan.

"Probably because you're so easy," said Kim. "Now cool it!" Ragan stood back and relaxed. Kim continued, "What we got here, gentlemen, is a mystery. We can't seem to identify who those people were who attacked this place this morning. There's a fellow in the hospital found in the airport parking lot and two others. Is there anything we can say to clear this up?" He turned to me.

"Wish I could help, but I really didn't get a good look at those fellows this morning and they weren't good conversationalists. Like Kim told you earlier, Mrs. Furman has been getting some weirdo threatening phone calls, so she asked me to help and I asked Kim to pitch in. Lucky we did or those guys would have wiped everyone out," I said.

"The question is what were they after?" demanded Ragan.

"We've been trying to figure that out and I think I've got it," I said. "They were probably illegals looking to hijack an airplane to get out of the country. Either that or they were trying to steal one of our freight shipments. Take your choice."

"I think there's a lot more," said Ragan. "We got a regular crime wave here and the trail leads right to you." He had a paper bag in his hand. "I've got something here for you to look at." He pulled a gun out of the bag.

It was unlike anything I'd ever seen. "Have you ever seen anything like this before?" he asked.

It was a small semi-automatic pistol-like weapon, like a U.S. Government issue Colt .45, with a longer barrel and bigger grip but it had a small canvas bag attached to the butt.

"This is the weapon those shooters used against you last night," he said. "It's an automatic pistol of some sort. This little canvas bag here holds one hundred fifty rounds of 9mm parabellum in a small neoprene belt that feeds through the butt of the weapon where the clip is supposed to be inserted. The neoprene belt feeds up and over the chamber, back down into the right side of the bag. I've never seen anything like it, but with a twelve inch barrel and a hundred fifty rounds, this is a lethal weapon and my boss don't like that it's being introduced into our city like this."

I took the weapon in my hands and said, "Yes, but what good is a hundred and fifty rounds if you can't hit anything. All you do then is scare the chickens."

"They got you, didn't they?" sneered Ragan.

"Yes, and while they were punching holes in the atmosphere we shut them down. You give that some thought, Detective. It's not how many shots you have, it's where you put the one you have in the chamber at the moment." I noticed that the gun had no markings.

"You talk big for a fellow who got ventilated. I think you were just lucky," said Ragan.

"Yes, I was lucky and I intend to stay that way. I'd advise you to get smart too, Detective, and stay alert. If you throw your weight around with these bozos the way you did here, you'll be dead before your next paycheck. These are bad actors," I said.

"I don't need your advice, buddy. I do whatever I hafta to get what I want," Ragan said.

"Well, that should be interesting, because that's the same philosophy these gunmen seem to have. It should be like the clash of the titans when you find them, just you against them. I'd like to see that," I said, as Ragan's neck and ears grew beet red again.

"Okay, that's enough," said Kim. "Take it easy."

"Sorry, couldn't resist. I have to visit the facilities," I said, handing the gun back. I struggled to stand and Kim helped me.

"I'm just gonna look around," said Ragan. "If I find you been hiding something you better be ready to explain it." He walked into the hangar and turned toward the office.

"I'll go with you, just in case you need help," said Kim, giving me a warning look as he took my arm and guided me away.

I limped into the hangar and found Mickey next to the King Air. He was bending a piece of metal to fit a hole in the engine cowling.

"Mickey, would you mind doing me a favor?" I said.

"Sure, no problem, Mr. O'Keefe. What is it?"

"I need the duffle bag out of my trunk. The car is out front," I said, handing him the keys.

"You should be more careful how you act with Bobby Ragan, Billy. His brother is the Chief of Police and he thinks he's bullet proof. I know how you feel about his type but he's not always rational so just be careful, okay?" Kim said.

"Yeah, sure. I guess I'm not really myself right now. It was a dumb act I pulled last night, getting shot that way. I could have let loose sooner and that would have given you time to come into it when they were still a good distance away," I said.

"You do what you have to when you're in a tight spot. There's never any going back after the first shot is fired. That's why you're as good as you are, O'Keefe. You took them by surprise and did the maximum amount of damage. You emptied three clips of 9 mm and five .44 Magnum loads. We would have taken them all down if that pickup hadn't showed up. So, now we have a couple of wounded prisoners who will eventually talk and that's on the plus side. In the words of my section chief when I was in Air Force intelligence, 'I can say with absolute certainty and without equivocation that last night was a definite maybe on the win side.' He was never wrong so I thought I'd just pass that along to you," Kim said, slapping me on the back.

"So am I supposed to feel better now that you've given me a definite-maybe pep talk?" I asked, laughing.

"That's up to you, Billy. You know as well as I do that there are never any clear winners in this game, only survivors," he said.

The weather was fine as I looked out at the sea gulls strutting down the taxiway. Somehow they always managed to stay out of the way of the airplanes and the thought struck me that I should tell Willie Monk about them.

It would be dark shortly and we would be into another night of protecting Furman Airways. I had gotten more than I bargained for with the shootout that morning on the tarmac, but it was clear that we were in this to the end. I needed time to heal and a place to do it. Looking around, I found a good hiding place on an airplane, gave it some thought, and decided to do it. I could use the break anyway. So I took my duffle bag, waved at Kim, climbed aboard, found a comfortable seat and relaxed.

The SPD truck came and loaded the airplane, and I was almost asleep when Linda started the engines and took off on her Dallas run. Kim Woo was with Chief Detective Bobby Ragan prowling around the hangar.

"Where's that O'Keefe fella? I got some more questions for him," Ragan asked.

"I think he went to Texas," said Kim, the bemused smile turning to a grin.

Chapter Eighteen

THE SPD truck delivered its cargo of packages and crates as usual. I was waiting on board the aircraft, resting in the right seat. Linda was breathless as she strapped herself into the pilot's seat and started the engines. I watched as Pete Drurey jumped into the SPD panel truck and drove away.

"That detective is looking for you and he's spittin' mad," said Linda, a smile crossing her face as she concentrated on the gauges.

"He won't catch me unless he has wings," I said.

"He's mad enough, he may just sprout some," she said, turning on the radios, flipping switches and releasing the brakes all at once.

Linda called Ground Control and got clearance to taxi to the active runway. When she was ready, we were turned over to the tower controller and received clearance for takeoff. We rolled down the runway, heavy with fuel and freight. I noticed she was struggling with the wheel as the distance markers flicked past in the landing lights of the aircraft. At 3,000 feet, she hauled back on the yoke and yelled, "Give me a hand, will ya? The damn trim tab is stuck again." I grabbed the yoke on my side and pulled. There was too much down pressure on it but we managed to lift the nose and we were airborne by the time we passed the 6,000 foot marker.

"This is an old aircraft. It's happened before. I'll try a few things to see if it'll work better as soon as we level off. Just help me keep it in a climb until we have the altitude. Mickey keeps promising to fix it but he's got too much to do," she said, struggling with the wheel.

We leveled out at 9,500 feet and she worked on the trim tabs by rolling them back and forth. "Sometimes it jumps the track and if you back it up a little it drops back in." She jiggled the wheel back and forth until it worked.

"There, that'll do it. I should have checked it before we took off but it's always a big rush to get off the ground and stay on schedule."

A scattered cloud deck above us revealed a half moon rising in the east, stars above, and an occasional scattering of clouds below. The New York-New Jersey metro area stretched off ahead of us, blending with the Philadelphia lights off to our left as we continued to the southwest.

"We have good weather all the way tonight so we'll go VFR. The jet stream is pretty far north so we'll stay low until we're halfway, then we'll climb and catch a push from the northerly flow. We should average about three hundred knots if I play it right, so we'll be in Wichita by 11:30. This airplane is over twenty years old but it still steps right out. The newer models are bigger, faster, and more expensive. Dad bought this airplane for $150,000. It was a wreck but we rebuilt it. It has the big 715 hp, PT6A-36 engines, Pratt & Whitney. A new plane costs over four and a half million now," she explained, as she checked her maps.

Linda knew her stuff, and if a man wasn't distracted by her obvious beauty he would see that she was an excellent pilot as well. I reminded myself of how young she was and that I had a job to do. I sat back and relaxed, concentrating on the chart in front of me. My leg was hurting so I adjusted the seat to relieve the pressure. Then I took another pain killer and fell asleep.

I awoke to the changing tempo of the props and the reduced whine of the engines. We were letting down and everything was total darkness around us. Linda was talking on the radio, and both her face and the gauges on the instrument panel were bathed in a soft reddish light. I tried to orient myself by looking out the windows but our whole world existed there in the cockpit.

"We're approaching Wichita," said Linda. "You had a good nap."

We were leaving 18,000 feet in a slow descent of about 300 feet per minute. I'd done some night flying and I knew that it was vastly different from daytime flight. At night there are illusions of space and distance where pilots have become lost just because they couldn't judge the difference. We had radios and instruments and Linda was familiar with the area so I wasn't worried about being lost. She was talking on the radio so I put on my headset and listened.

"Center, this is Beech Twenty-One Alpha, outta seventeen and canceling IFR. Thanks, fellas," she said.

"Roger, sweetheart, it's been a pleasure. Ya'll come again, now, ya hear?" said the voice on the other end.

"Roger that and so long for now." Linda flashed me a smile. "Fella asked me out for a date. His supervisor better not listen to that tape. He'll fire that controller."

"Do you know him?" I asked.

"I've talked to him before. These center controllers are on real crazy schedules. They work different hours every week, so I get this fella about once every two or three weeks. He's really hot to meet me but I can't take the time. Hell, if I stopped for every guy who gave me a whistle, I'd be goin' backwards most of the time."

"You must get a lot of attention from the boys," I said. I noticed her accent had thickened as we progressed southwest.

"Yeah, but I can't say I enjoy it much any more. Mom is a good lookin' woman and I guess she gave some of it to me." The accent was pure southwest twang by now.

"I'd say you improved on it," I said without knowing why.

"Thanks, I'm trying to be the best at what I do, not manipulate my way to the top with my good looks. Mom is one of the best woman pilots in the country. I just want to be as good. Believe me, she's not an easy act to follow," she said.

"You could always try the airlines," I ventured.

"Yeah, I could and probably will someday. Maybe real soon if you don't find Dad and bring him home. It's hard without him. You are going to find him, aren't you?" she asked, a challenge in her voice.

"I'll try. I've got some things to check out first," I said.

"Like what?" She was looking at me hard, her

expression not friendly. "Why can't you just go find him and bring him home? Then we could get on with our lives. What's more important than bringing Dad home?" she said.

"I explained this all to your mother. She's satisfied with what I'm doing," I said.

"Yeah? Well I'm not Mom and I don't get it. Why are you here and not back there looking for my daddy? What do you hope to find out here? They could kill him and there's nothing any of us could do." She wasn't crying and she wasn't angry, just talking tough.

"Okay, Linda. Tell me why these people are trying to take over Furman Airways? Why did they kidnap your father and sabotage your airplanes? There's a lot that just doesn't make sense here. I could open the wrong door or step into a trap, if I move too fast, and then they would kill your father. Believe me, I've worked against these types before. As long as they need your father alive, he'll be alive. Once they have what they want, they'll kill him ... and probably the rest of you as well," I said.

She was quiet. We were out of 10,000 feet now, still descending, and I could see some lights on the ground.

"There are some questions I can find answers to out here, Linda. For instance, what's in those wooden crates back there?" I asked.

"Ball bearings!" she snapped. "You can read the damn printing on the boxes, can't you?"

"I can read, but tell me why they're shipping so many ball bearings to Texas. Where do they go? Who buys them, and why does the man who says he's a DEA agent deliver them to you, and why does he wait until you close the cargo door and start the engines before he drives away in an SPD truck?" I said.

"You say that fella's a DEA agent?" she asked.

"He says he is, but I don't believe it and if he is, then he's doing something that doesn't make sense and it's probably illegal," I said.

"Like what?" she asked. I had her interest.

"Like shipping boxes south in a business where everything else is traveling north. When we get on the ground, I want a look at those crates and what's in them," I said.

"We're not supposed to open anything. There are very strict rules about that," she said, adjusting the throttles.

"Sometimes we have to bend the rules, especially when you're dealing with criminals who don't play by anyone's rules," I said.

"Okay, but be careful. If they see a damaged crate or box at the other end, I'm in big trouble," she said.

"I'll try to keep you out of trouble, young lady," I said.

"Oh! Mr. O'Keefe! Your middle name is 'Trouble' with a capital 'T,' and you are a puzzle, but I guess I'm glad you're here because we need all the help we can get with this mess." She keyed her mike, "Mid-Continent, this is Beech Six Four Two One Alpha, over."

"Beech Six Four Two one Alpha, Mid-Continent go ahead." The controller's voice was crystal clear, but he sounded tired.

"Roger, Beech Twenty-One Alpha is thirty east, landing, we've got the numbers," she said.

"Twenty-One Alpha, report right base."

I waited a minute, watching the lights of Wichita slide under the nose. "You're very professional," I said.

"It's what I do and I want to be the best," she said.

"Same here, Babe!" I echoed, in a whisper.

"What do you mean?" she asked.

"I'm a professional. It's what I do and I am the best there is."

"We'll see," she said, looking at me with a smile.

We landed, not using much of the runway, and taxied to Engine-Reworks in a hangar on the far side of the field. We were met by a crew and Linda called for fuel on the Unicom frequency. Before the props stopped we were being unloaded and refueled. I found movement with my leg possible but painful. I moved to the back of the airplane and pulled one of the wooden crates out of the cargo area, as the crew unloaded the broken engine. I picked out a screwdriver from my duffle bag and opened the crate, all the while checking for booby-traps, seals or trips that would tip someone off that the crate had been opened, but I didn't find any. The inside of the crate was wrapped in a heavy oil-resistant brown paper neatly folded to protect the contents and I opened the wrapper.

I can't say I was surprised: blown away would be more like it. What I was looking at was one of the most unusual pieces of workmanship I've ever seen. There, before my very eyes, was an automatic pistol much like the ones used by the attackers the morning before at Furman Airways, only this one was even better. It was your basic semi-automatic type pistol frame with standard grips, trigger, and safety. The hammer was visible but was faired into the frame so it wouldn't snag on anything. The barrel, about eighteen inches long, had a vented gas-operated mechanism mounted below it.

A flip-out handle on the barrel swung to both sides so the weapon could be fired either left or right handed. A folding wire stock lay beside it, and a small canvas bag full of 9mm parabellum belt-fed ammo was there to be attached to the butt of the weapon. The gun was probably lethal up to fifty feet and effective up to a hundred feet. The imprint on the slide and frame read "MAK II" and there were no other markings. I checked the rest of the crate and found more of the same under layers of heavy paper, packed in a staggered fashion to take advantage of space, all complete with canvas ammo bags and ready to go.

The activity in the front of the aircraft had ceased and Linda came back to where I was sitting. The expression on her face was one of disapproval at first, probably because I'd broken the rules and opened an SPD crate, but that changed when she saw the weapons.

"Oh my gosh! Where did you find that? What is it?" she said.

"That's a ball bearing, babe, and I'm Santa Claus," I said.

"Some ball bearing, Mr. O'Keefe. Are there more?" she asked, a shocked expression on her face.

"An even dozen, all with ammo bags and folding butt stocks, ready to go. A squad of rebels could start a war with these. You could walk down the street with this weapon fully loaded, under your serape and no one would know you had it: instant revolution," I said.

We were in the back of the aircraft waiting for the ground crews to finish refueling and Linda was in a state of disbelief. "But why? Aren't there enough guns in the world? Why ship these things in our airplanes? What does it all mean?" she said.

"I can only guess but I don't think any responsible person in our government knows about this. It may explain the reason for your father's kidnapping and the attempt to take over Furman Airways. This weapon wouldn't be used in jungle or mountain warfare. It's best suited to urban guerrilla warfare. I'll bet that somebody has a timetable with a deadline, hence the rush to acquire Furman Airways right away," I said, repacking the crate.

"You mean someone is planning a revolution?" she asked.

"I don't know, but look at it this way. You're a drug cartel leader in South America and you want protection so you can produce and ship your product to market, but Uncle Sam's narcs keep closing you down using helicopters and riverboats armed with M60 machine guns. They have you outgunned, out-maneuvered, and on the run, so what do you do? Go to the cities and arm the street gangs. Take over the country and kick out the Yanks, and how do you pay for it? You ship drugs north and guns south. It's not a new concept," I said. Linda shivered as if it were cold but I was sweating.

I took two of the weapons and put them aside, closed the crate and replaced the eight screws holding the top. I decided to restack the crates and put the one I'd opened on the bottom when I noticed something.

The screws in the top of the crates were all turned the same way, parallel to the boards on the top. I checked the other crates and they were the same. The slots on all screws were aligned exactly right and left. This wasn't a seal or trip wire but it wasn't as obvious either. I went back to the crate I'd opened and adjusted the screws so the slots matched those of the other crates. Twenty crates with twelve weapons each equaled two hundred forty weapons. Would they miss two? I really didn't care but the potential was awesome. Two hundred forty times one hundred fifty rounds per canvas bag equaled what? I did the calculations, showing it to Linda as she started the engines.

"Thirty-six thousand rounds per load? That's incredible," she said. "And to think, we carry twenty or more of these crates on almost every trip, three times a week."

"Scary, isn't it? Do you know where these crates are going?" I asked as we taxied out to the active runway.

"The paperwork just says Hi-Tec Ball Bearings, 3697 Old Galveston Road, Houston, Texas. The SPD truck will meet us at the freight terminal at Houston Intercontinental Airport. Where they take the stuff after that is anyone's guess. I'm always too busy to notice who's doing what around me." Linda called the tower for clearance.

"And that's why they want your flight operation. If they shipped by normal freight, the crates would be subject to periodic inspection. This way they bypass that, and Houston's an international port so it's simple to smuggle 'Ball Bearings' to Colombia or anyplace else."

"That address, Old Galveston Road, isn't far from the

Port of Houston Ship Channel, but don't the customs people check stuff like this before it's shipped?" she asked.

"We're not as diligent about what's shipped out as we are about what comes in. Customs is on watch in places like Boston where shipments of arms to Ireland are occasionally spotted. You can be sure these criminals did their homework before picking Houston."

We received our clearance and took off for Dallas. The trip took us about an hour and fifteen minutes and it was after 1:00 A.M. when we touched down at Love Field, Dallas. The SPD truck met us and I stayed out of sight in the cockpit while Linda saw to the unloading of some packages. We picked up mailbags for Houston and were on our way in no time. Linda spoke her mind as we climbed out of Dallas.

"I've got a real funny feeling about all this. Just knowing what's back there makes me want to puke. I guess I've led a pretty sheltered life. I went to TCU over in Fort Worth," she said, pointing to our right as the aircraft was climbing, "and I thought I was grown up when I graduated two years ago. I've been working for my folks ever since. I've heard about illegal drugs and arms shipments and I've even known some people who were heavy into drugs, but I just steered clear of them and went on about my business. Now, shipping guns to rebels in South America, wow, that's right out of the movies."

"This is the real thing," I said, "and there's nothing glamorous about it. In the drugs-for-arms business there are no ethics or morals, no promises kept, no good guys versus bad guys. Everyone in this business is a bad guy and you can't afford to believe anything they tell you. Believe only what you see and trust only what you know to be true. The rest is baloney and could get you killed."

"You sound cynical," she said pulling the power back and leveling off at 10,500 feet.

"I've seen too much of this sort of thing and I have the scars to prove it," I said, dialing the airway radial from the Dallas Vortac.

"So, tell me something, old man," she said emphasizing the old, as the red lights of the instrument panel reflected off the smile on her face. "Can I trust you, Mr. O'Keefe?"

"Follow your heart, my child," I said. "Follow your heart," and I pointed to the needle on the VOR display as it settled on course.

Chapter Nineteen

THE flight from Dallas to Houston took less than an hour. Fifteen minutes on the ground and we were unloaded. I watched the SPD driver transfer the crates but there was nothing out of the ordinary. He didn't even look at the tops of the wooden crates. He was just in a big hurry. I wondered if he was a DEA agent as well or if he was even connected with Morton Bolinsky and the drug cartels. Just how far did their influence reach, and how powerful were they outside their own backyards? I was sure I'd soon find out. The two machine pistols where in a paper bag under the co-pilot's seat, where I was sitting, covered casually with a half-opened aeronautical chart.

"We have to drop off these mail sacks over there across from that American Airlines terminal," said Linda. "From there we can go directly to the hotel and get some sleep. I could go for a shower too. This Houston air is always hot and muggy."

"Maybe I should stay with the aircraft. I don't want anything to happen to it," I said, thinking of the two weapons under my seat.

"Don't worry. These airport security guards are tough and they don't mess around down here. I'll tell them we've been having trouble," she said.

Houston looked like one big electric light bulb from our balcony on the tenth floor of the Regency Hotel. We had adjoining rooms. Linda said good night and locked the door from her side. I took a quick shower, trying to keep my leg and head bandages dry but I didn't do a very good job. I lay down on top of the bed and tried to relax, but I was so wired I couldn't sleep. So I turned on the TV and watched a local all night talk show.

Eventually, I dropped off to sleep and only vaguely remembered Linda crawling into bed and snuggling up beside me. She said something about being alone and how would I like company, and that's about all I remembered, until later, when we made love and that I would never forget. She was young and hungry, not greatly experienced but willing to learn and eager to please. I was thrown from one extreme to the other between the ecstasy of love and the jolting pain of my wounded leg and head. No complaints, mind you, but a lot of guilt.

We slept, and when we awoke again it was still early morning and the Texas sun was up and hot. I was feeling groggy from the long trip, the short sleep, and the intense love making. The painkillers were wearing off and reality was setting in. I had work to do and I was in no shape to do it. Linda was bouncing around like a teenager, making semi-sarcastic remarks about "getting my old butt" in gear and could she get a "senior citizen's discount" on my room.

"I just want to get out of Texas, before they find out you're underage," I quipped. "I hear they hang a man down here for messing around with a girl who's not legal."

"You should be so lucky as to die that way. I'll be glad to testify at your trial that you gave a good account of yourself. At least that would keep your reputation intact," she said, laughing.

"I really appreciate your loyalty. Seriously, Linda, what happened between us was great but where can we go from here?" I asked.

"We're grown up people. We can see each other any time. I really like you, O'Keefe. I know about your friend, Connie, and that's all right with me. I'm not looking to take you over full time. I just want a piece of you, now and then, okay?" She put her arms around me and planted a big juicy kiss on my mouth.

"Yes ... sure ... just let me know when reality sets in again. I'm running low on oxygen," I said.

We grabbed a quick breakfast in the hotel snack bar. I called Furman Airways and told Kim to call me back from a pay phone that was away from the hangar and he did.

"All's well here. Had a quiet night. Billy Jean's worried about you and her daughter, not that she doesn't trust you but she's been asking questions. Wants to know how trustworthy you really are," he said.

"Tell her not to worry. We had separate rooms and we did not, I repeat, did not have breakfast in bed. Geeze! Cut me some slack, Kim. I'm a wounded man. Billy Jean has known me a long time. Besides, I've got work to do, you two-faced son of Wong," I said.

"Me thinks the man doth protest too much," said Kim, "and that's Woo, not Wong."

"Wait until I get back. I'll show you what happens when you doubt a friend's trust," I said.

"I thought you were a wounded man?" he jibed.

"Don't push me, short man. I can heal between here and there."

Kim said John Chusak called from Chicago and said he couldn't trace the two DEA agents, Pete and Jake, and that maybe they were independent contractors. Kim doubted that and was checking with some of his old Pentagon contacts to find out who they were. Chusak said SPD was a legitimate company and probably didn't know anything about the guns for drugs deal. He said Chief Bobby Ragan had been around and was very upset because I was gone. He was threatening to issue warrants for my arrest and cut out my liver when he found me. Jack Sullivan was having a good time helping Billy Jean organize and run an airline, and Connie called to say her father was better and out of danger. I said I'd be back in the early afternoon and hung up.

There was another phone call I had to make but I decided to wait. Linda was checked out and had an airport limousine waiting.

"Come on, Bill, we have to meet the trucks by 8:30," she said, looking better than ever.

We made it just in time, and I made my other call from a pay phone in the airfreight terminal as the SPD driver helped load the airplane. I dialed the number for the Houston District FBI office and asked to speak to the agent in charge. A man came on the line and identified himself as Agent Carl Watson. I told him my name and where I was from. I told him about the machine pistols and gave him the Houston address of Hi-Tec Ball Bearings.

"I'd like to talk to you in person and take a written statement, Mr. O'Keefe," said Watson.

"Sorry, I'm leaving town and I probably won't be back. I have a lot of work to do on the other end. Be careful of this one, Carl. There may be another agency involved and they may be dirty," I warned.

I told him about Pete and Jake and their claim of being DEA agents. I mentioned Morton Bolinsky and got a "Wow" response. Carlos Montalbo got a "Son of a bitch." I told him I needed time and space to protect Furman Airways but I said nothing about Tony Furman.

"I'll cooperate in any way I can but I want Furman Airways kept clean on this one. They didn't know what was going on. I'll be in contact with you when and if I get more." I hung up and limped to the aircraft, which was waiting fully loaded and fueled.

"We've gotta go, Bill. I have a schedule to meet. Sorry, but the fun's over for now," she said.

"Not really, pretty lady. The fun is probably just beginning here in Houston," I said.

Linda was in a hurry. She gave me a quizzical glance and helped me up the stairs into the cabin. We pulled the stairs up and locked the door. As she started the engines, I looked through the packages the SPD driver had delivered and found several addressed to Fernandes Nurseries in Southold, New York. I took three of the smaller ones and went forward where Linda was talking to the tower. She picked up her clearance from ground control to taxi to the active runway, released the brakes and we were moving. There was no delay for takeoff and as we broke ground, Linda asked for an immediate "right turn out on course" and we were on our way.

"Every minute counts on this leg," she said. "This airplane has long range tanks but it's still a long haul from Houston to Newark. We've got some thunder bumpers along the way that could push us south, so what I'm going to do is point us northeast, get a kick in the tail from the Gulf winds, and make a couple of hundred miles north of our normal track. I can go maybe 25,000 feet with this load so I'll try to pick up an IFR clearance someplace south of St. Louis. Most of the storms are over Kentucky and Tennessee moving northeast, so we've gotta kick ass to make it," she said, and we did.

"Sorry if I held you up. I had to check in with some people to make sure everything was all right. I talked with Kim Woo and he said everything was quiet there but your mother is worried about me taking advantage of you. I told him we had separate rooms," I said.

"I don't know about you, Mr. O'Keefe, but I think what you and I do is our business and I'd like to keep it that way. I'm tired of being alone and my mom will just have to get used to the fact I'm a grown woman, and if you're the man I want, that's my business," she said.

I didn't argue with her. It wouldn't do any good. Things had really changed since I was young. In the old days the boy asked the girl out and he made the first moves. The girl responded in whatever way she chose and the mating dance proceeded from there. Now, the woman has all the options open to her that a man used to have and the dance is not so simple. I consoled myself with the thought that this was a one-time adventure, and when we returned Linda would probably find someone younger and more exciting.

These thoughts occupied my mind as we passed Shreveport and then Little Rock. We had a thirty-knot tail wind at 17,000 feet and just as Linda had predicted, we encountered a line of thunderstorms growing to the south and southeast of Louisville. She requested an IFR clearance to New York and we climbed to flight level two three zero (FL230) where the jet stream was kicking along at fifty-five knots out of the southwest. We detoured north and east of the buildups and managed to stay in the clear all the way with the help of some very understanding center controllers. I spent my time cross checking our position and tuning in the radials of the respective VORs on the twin set of radios, while using the GPS as backup.

Somewhere north of Columbus I remembered the packages I had brought forward and set about opening them, slitting the bottoms so the tops would remain untouched. The first two had the same weird looking roots or bulbs that I found in the trunk of the Ford that morning on the highway in Rye. I debated about opening the third one but did it anyway, and much to my surprise found something different.

"Is that what I think it is?" asked Linda.

"I don't know unless I open it but it looks very much like cocaine." I punctured the small plastic bag with my pocketknife and tasted it. "Yuck! This is raw, uncut cocaine. I'm no expert but I'd say this is about as strong as it gets. The stuff in those other boxes is some sort of mescaline or peyote; you know, mushrooms. Kim seems to know a lot about them. They're worth a lot of bucks on the street but not as much as this white powder," I said.

"There's some clear tape back there we use to repair damaged packages. You better use it to re-seal those boxes," Linda said.

I moved back into the cabin and did as she suggested, putting the boxes back where I found them. We were at flight level two five zero (FL250) deviating around gigantic blue-black thunder cells. Below was a tumult of clouds, rain, and lightening. The power of a fully matured thunderstorm can never be completely described. We were a miniscule little flyspeck in the middle of a boiling cauldron of cloud, wind, and rain. I had to admit to myself that I was ... well, slightly uneasy. Okay, make that a lot apprehensive, and between the pain in my head and leg and the drugs, I wasn't feeling well.

"Are you scared, Mr. O'Keefe?" Linda teased.

"No, of course not," I said. "Why do you ask?"

"You look a little green around the gills. Don't worry, Bill, this is a picnic compared to what can happen. So just sit back, relax, and leave the driving to me, big boy." She put her hand on my thigh just above the wound. Just kidding, Bill. We'll be down in an hour and we can relax and pick up where we left off." She paused and looked at me, "That is, if you still want to."

"I'm looking forward to it," I said, putting my hand on hers. What else could I say to a woman who held my life in her hands?

We kept our IFR flight plan all the way into the

New York TCA (Terminal Control Area). We landed at Newark airport, which can only be compared to walking through a swarm of bees and trying to find a place to sit. Finding a parking place for an afternoon game at Yankee Stadium would be a piece of cake compared to landing at Newark. It wasn't just the twists and turns they put us through in the air maneuvering to final approach. On the ground, there were a number of obstacles to avoid, like construction vehicles, delivery trucks, detours for disabled airplanes and closed taxiways. We taxied to the freight terminal where we were met by the SPD truck, and the driver was not happy.

"You're late, sweetheart. Where the hell have you been?" he said.

"Thunderstorms, dimwit! You should try them on for size sometime, buster." She tossed a large heavy box at him from the cargo door of the aircraft. "Heads up," she yelled as she grabbed another.

I waited until the truck was gone and went back to help her pull up the stairs and close the door.

"I'll get this if you want to start the engines," I said.

Linda smiled and said, "Thanks, it's nice to be with a real gentleman for a change."

She went forward to the cockpit. I had the stairs pulled halfway up when a hand reached up, grabbed my arm and jerked me right through the door opening and onto the asphalt, flat on my keister. I rolled over, painfully, and the hand grabbed me by my hair. I came face to face with the ugly countenance of DEA agent Jake Gibbons. I hooked the back of his leg with my hand and pulled hard, dumping him on his back. Then I stood and reached for his hair, meaning to grind the jerk's face into the tarmac, when someone hit me on the head from behind. It hurt but I was still conscious. I turned and looked straight into the menacing coal black eyes of Humberto Rada, and then he hit me again. The last thing I remembered was the whine of the engines as the turbines spooled up and the props chased them to a howling screaming climax.

Chapter Twenty

I had the granddaddy of all splitting headaches and I couldn't see straight. Everything was blurred. My hands and legs were tied with some sort of twine and I was on a cold cement floor in an old smelly basement room. I couldn't move. The only light came from a small barred window high up on the old granite foundation and I could hear traffic outside. There were voices and children laughing and screaming in the distance. I tried to remember what happened but I couldn't put it all together. I closed my eyes and tried to concentrate on making the pain go away but that didn't work.

I fell asleep again and when I woke up I could hear voices on the other side of one of the walls. I scooted over and looked through a hole in the wall. A single light hung over a table where three men, Humberto Rada, Miguel Rada, and my DEA buddy Jake Gibbons, were mixing and weighing white powder. Miguel was filling and sealing a pile of smaller packages with an iron. They were talking in Spanish, too fast for me to follow the conversation. My Glock was hanging in its holster off the back of Jake Gibbons' chair.

Another man came in. At first I couldn't see him but I recognized the voice. It was Mr. DEA himself, Pete Drurey. He and Jake had a conversation to one side out of my line of sight, then they went out and I heard them outside the door to my room. I scooted back to my place on the floor and lay down, pretending to be out of it, which wasn't far from the truth. I heard a key being inserted in the lock and the door opened.

"He ain't moved," said Jake. "Maybe he's dead."

"He better not be, you big jerk. The man wants him alive, for now," said Pete.

"Yeah, awright, but why? What the hell good is he to us?"

"You should know without me tellin' you, Jake. We gotta find out what he knows and who he's talked to. You'll never be anything but muscle if you don't start using your head," Pete said.

"You never complained before when you needed my muscle. Where would you be without me, huh? Think that over, Pete. It's my muscle what got us here, right?" Jake said.

"I'm thinking about it, Jake. I'm thinking about it real hard. So, while I'm trying not to forget how we got here, why don't you sit Mr. O'Keefe up and see if he's still able to talk after what you and Humberto did to him," Pete said.

They picked me up and dumped me in a chair. I pretended to be unconscious. For that I got slapped a few times on the side of the head.

"Thanks, Jake, I really needed that," I mumbled, opening my eyes.

"Drop dead, jerk," he sneered, bringing his hand back for another slap.

"That'll do, Jake. We don't wanna knock him out

again before we get a chance to talk to him," said Pete.
"

The questions went on for about two hours, with Jake stepping in occasionally to slap me around just to remind everyone who was in charge. I really don't like being hit on the side of my head because that's where my ears are and it hurts to be cuffed in the ears. It leaves your head ringing, you get dizzy and nauseous, and sometimes you fall out of the chair onto the cold cement floor and then Jake has to pick you up and wait until you come to again. That's the best part because it gives you time to rest and plan your next offensive. I was getting tired of hitting Jake's hand with my head but I figured Pete and Jake would give up before I did. Still the questions continued.

"Who did you tell about the mushrooms?"

"Who did you tell about the guns?"

"Does anyone else know about the cocaine shipments?"

"Two guns were missing out of a crate in Houston! Did you take them? Where are they?"

"Does your little girlfriend know about this?"

"Who are you working for?"

"Who's the old geezer who tied up our technician in that apartment?"

"Who's the slant-eyed bastard who wasted our guys at the airport?"

"Who tipped you off about the attack at the airport yesterday?"

"Did you tell Detective Ragan anything?"

"Where did you get the money to buy out the note on Furman Airways?"

So it went until they repeated themselves and slapped me so many times it no longer mattered. Then they quit. I was sitting slumped over in the chair when they said something about dinner. They locked the door and left me alone. The light in the next room went out and there I was with no one to play with. I was going to miss Jake a lot. He was a real fun guy, the kind you just love to invite to a party, especially if it was a Ku Klux Klan or Neo-Fascist party. I'd have to remember him the next time I threw a bash for all my friends.

"Remember that, O'Keefe." I said out loud. "Don't forget to invite old Jake to your next party," and I fell out of the chair again.

It was real dark when I came to and I was lying on the floor. Some outside light from the street came through the window but not much. No one seemed to be around in the next room, so I tried to stand up and collect my thoughts. I found it was too much effort so I scooted over against the stone wall.

I put my hands down behind me and lifted my butt, scooting along a few inches at a time. At the wall, I put my hands down for what I thought would be the last time and felt the jagged edge of a bottle crunch under my weight, cutting the palm of my left hand. That was all I needed, more cuts, more bleeding, more pain. The wound in my leg was bleeding and hurting more than ever and I was out of pain killers. They wouldn't have helped anyway because I was overdosed on pain.

I rested and tried to think about my situation. It

didn't make sense for me to be there, tied up, bleeding and bruised in some dark damp cellar, sitting on broken glass. I tried to close my eyes, not easy since they were bruised and swollen. Even my eyelashes hurt.

My mind finally sorted it all out. Find something less damaging to sit on. So I felt around until I found a clear spot along the wall and I sat there and rested for a while watching the little furry rat creatures crawl around sniffing at my legs and feet. They didn't chew on me, so I left them alone.

That's my philosophy, live and let live. I gave it some more thought and decided the broken bottle wasn't such a bad idea after all. I found it and started working at the twine that bound my wrists. It wasn't as easy as I thought it would be and I had to rest several times before I got my hands loose. I couldn't do much with them because they were numb and stiff. I finally managed to loosen my legs when I got the circulation working again. Then came standing up, which took another fifteen minutes.

So there I was back on my feet, as the saying goes, and no place to go. I pulled the chair over next to the stone foundation wall and checked the bars on the window. They were set in holes drilled into the granite blocks that formed the window opening. No getting out that way. I checked the door but got no encouragement there either.

It was a large, metal-clad affair with a bar latch on the outside and a very sophisticated modern dead bolt installed over that. I had no tools to work on something that heavy. I did have my sports jacket, however, and in the left outside pocket was the wad of plastik explosive which

I took from the IFR trainer that Riccardo Fernandes was trying to sabotage in the hangar at Furman Airways.

The square lump of explosive was flattened out from all the rolling around on the cement floor. In the right pocket was the blasting cap, its yellow and green wires neatly coiled just as I'd left them when I placed it in my pocket after showing it to Donald Long. I was really lucky it hadn't detonated when Jake was exercising his muscles on me. But there it was and there was the plastik explosive and there I was in a locked room. I love locked room mysteries, as long as I have the explosives.

I found an electric outlet on the wall next to the room where the other guys had been packaging their cocaine, removed the plate and tested the wires for power. I got a good zap. I freed the wires from the socket and hooked up the green wire of the blasting cap, leaving the yellow one free. I stuck the blasting cap into the plastik explosive and stuffed the whole thing into one of the holes in the wall. I tied lengths of twine together until I had a piece long enough to do the job. Then I bared the live wire and scraped it with a quarter until the copper was bright and shiny. I pulled it out and laid the twine across it, tied the twine to the loose yellow blasting cap wire, crouched in the opposite corner and pulled. Nothing happened the first two times. It took a third try before I got contact, but when I did it was a real blast.

As the dust settled I walked into the next room which was bathed in white powder. The blast had destroyed the whole wall as well as the entire pile of cocaine on the table in the next room and had set fire to the wood ceiling and walls. My hearing was wiped out and I felt like

I was walking in a vacuum. My pistol was in the corner so I picked it up and strapped it on my left ankle. The Special Forces knife that I had borrowed from Kim was on the floor so I took that too. I went up the stairs and came out in a hallway with a door to the right that led outside.

The air was thick with smoke and cocaine dust, a particularly obnoxious combination, and I was feeling no pain by the time I reached the street. It seems I'd discovered a new way of sniffing coke. First of all, put your powder in a pile on a table, then blow the room up and take a deep breath. I must have been really high, because I thought it was so funny I just stood there and laughed. People were staring as they passed me on the sidewalk while others were escaping the building carrying all their earthly belongings. I didn't think they would like it if they found out I was the one who started the fire so I decided to "depart the scene" as the saying goes.

Chapter Twenty-one

I was on a street in a city. The cars had New York license plates. The buildings were in poor condition and as I walked, I saw that the streets were filthy with garbage and abandoned cars. Actually, the street down which I was walking looked like a war zone. My brain began to clear as I walked. I was dodging broken bottles, burned mattresses, broken furniture, and homeless drunks. I turned a corner and came face to face with a group of teenage boys hanging out on the front steps of a tenement house. There were maybe seven or eight of them. I tried to turn around and go back the way I came, but they surrounded me before I reached the corner.

"Hey, dude! What you doin', huh?" said a tall boy, stepping in front of me.

"Yeah, old man, you in our territory, man. What you doin' here?"

"You deaf or somethin', old man?"

"Hey, he's all beat up. Look at him, man, he's all bloody."

Half of them were black, others were white with a few shades in between, and their ages ran from maybe thirteen or fourteen up to twenty. I didn't really want to tangle with these kids right now but it looked as if I didn't have a choice.

"Look, uhh, fellows. I'm just a bit lost here. Can you point me toward a telephone?" I asked.

"Hey man, it talks. Look it that ... it wants a telephone," one of them said with a heavy accent.

"Ain't no telephones in this neighborhood, man. We tore 'em all out. Right, Julio baby?"

They all had the same haircut. Shaved on the sides with a spiked ridge down the middle. Their shirts read "VULTURES" across their backs.

"Yeah, man, hey, we needed the change, man. Ain't no telephones left."

"You got any money, dude?" The tall one they called Julio pushed me and pulled a knife. "Give me your money now man or I'll cut you up!" he said, with the emphasis on the "up".

He put his hand on my chest. I instinctively grabbed it and twisted, breaking the wrist and turning him sideways. I tripped him, and stomped on his neck when he hit the pavement. I palmed the next one in the chin as he came at me, and stepped aside as another took a try at my back. I kicked one in the crotch and chopped one across the nose. They were on me like a pack of hyenas. I managed to get my back to the wall in a corner between the building and the steps so they had to come straight on at me.

I kicked as best I could and chopped when I could, poked one in the eye and broke a couple of noses. It was not a job to be proud of. They were mostly just kids, but each one had a knife and one came up with a gun and shot two of his buddies. He ran out of ammo and never did hit me. One of the boys who caught a bullet in the leg was down on one knee yelling.

"Manny, you bird shit ... you A-hole ... you shot the wrong people, turd head! Man, you crazy or somethin'? Huh? Shit ...!" he said, and then he passed out.

There were only three of them standing now but I was taking no chances. I went over to Manny, took the gun away and stuck it in my pocket. I turned and walked away and wisely they didn't follow.

I wandered around like a drunken fool until I came to a wide, well lit thoroughfare with stores. A sign half way down the block indicated an all night cafeteria was open and I went inside. I had no money in my pockets but I did have a fifty-dollar bill tucked into my shoe for emergencies, so I ordered a hamburger and a cup of coffee.

"Hey look, mack. I can't change that," said the man behind the counter, holding the fifty up to the light. I put the gun on the counter, pointed at it. I pushed it over to him.

"I'm sorry, it's all I have." How about a trade for the gun?" I said, leaning on the counter.

"What the hell happened to you, anyway, mister?" he asked.

"Got mugged, I guess ... I just need something to eat ... and a telephone," I muttered, as I went through my pockets.

"Hey! Rivera," yelled the cook, calling to a young man at a corner table. "Got a minute?" He said, pushing the gun aside.

The young man came strolling across the restaurant

wearing a long brown overcoat matching his skin color. He wore a broad brimmed hat, like a Stetson, and a large gold chain around his neck. Gold earrings and a gold nose stud made the statement complete.

"What you want, Harry?" He looked at me and then at the cook.

"Can you break a fifty, Rivera? That's all this gent has."

"Is it a good one? I don't wan' no funny money, mister."

I gave him the fifty and he held it to the light, rubbed it and checked his fingers for ink, scratched the face of Jackson and turned it over and over. Finally, he seemed satisfied.

"You wan' a fix, man? How bout a gig, huh? Nice little chick?"

"No, thanks," I said. "I need food and a telephone. I have to get back home."

"Okay then but you don' look so good, ya know?" as he peeled off four ten-dollar bills. "I get me a commission," he said, yellow decayed teeth showing through his smile as he eyed the gun.

"Okay," I said, "and thank you." He nodded, grabbing the gun and walked back to the table in a corner where he'd been sitting.

I ate my hamburger and drank the hot black coffee and tried to figure things out. I finally decided I had to get some help and soon. I was about done in. I went to the counter and waited for the cook.

"Look, I'm in trouble, as if you couldn't tell. I need a telephone or a cab. I need a ride, okay? I'm willing to pay. I just ... well ..." I wasn't making sense. "I don't know where I am ..." I said.

He looked at me and shook his head. "You up-towners always get in trouble. What are you, anyway, a stockbroker? Just looking for a little action and got more than you bargained for, right?" he said.

"No, not really," I said in an even low voice, trying to control my rage. "Like I said, I got mugged and I wasn't looking for action. I was in Newark Airport and I God damned got mugged and now I don't know where I am and I need to get home. I just need some help from somebody who is not out to rob me or kill me or mess me up, okay?" I spoke very slowly, my hands flat on the counter.

"Yeah, sure ... okay, buddy. I gotcha. Well to begin with you are in the Bronx, East 161st Street and 3rd Avenue right over there. I don't know how you got here but that's where you're at." He turned and yelled again, "Hey, Rivera! Got a minute?"

"Yeah, man, what is it?" Rivera came swaggering over. A young black woman in a miniskirt had joined him at his table. "You got another fifty for me or somethin'?"

I explained my situation again and Rivera listened. "So you sayin' you need a ride to this Airport and that's all and you're willin' to pay for it?" He looked at me like he could not believe I was for real.

"Yes," I said.

"Hey, my girl Marty, says some dude in a gray sports jacket with blood all over him messed up the Vultures over near the park. You got any ideas about that?" He looked at me closely.

"Are they friends of yours?" I asked.

"No way, mister. The Vultures is a mean bunch. They ain't friends of nobody, no how, and from what Marty say, there ain't but one or two of them left," he said.

"Three, actually, unless one of them succumbed after the encounter," I said. "They were just kids. They pulled knives on me. I don't like it when people do that. One had a gun. He shot two of his own. I just want to go home, all right? I'm tired of people trying to mug me. Sorry I bothered you. I'll call a cab." I started to walk away.

"No, mister, you don't have to go," said Rivera. "I'll drive you. Cost you two bills. You won't get a cab to come up here and besides, no cabbie would let you in his car lookin' like that. It's a slow Saturday night. I could use the break. Okay? Two bills. What say?"

"I'll have to get it on the other end," I said. "I don't have it on me but my friends have it. I'm good for it."

"Okay, yeah, I think you are. Them Vultures, mister, they were good for nothin', but you now, you are somethin' else," he said, slapping me on the shoulder. More pain. "Hey, mister, what's your name anyway?"

"O'Keefe," I said cautiously. "William O'Keefe."

"Yeah? No kiddin'. Hey, ain't you the dude the man's been askin' around about? You some sort of private eye or somethin'?" he said.

"No, I do insurance claims. I'm sort of semi-employed, if you know what I mean," I said.

"Yeah, man, me too," said Rivera, leading the way out to the curb. "We better get you outta here fast before the man, he get wind of where you are."

"Who's this man?" I asked.

"Can't say. I don't mess with him and he don't pay no attention to me. I run my girls and pay my dues and stay outta sight. You jest got more important and a lot more dangerous. Maybe I should get me, say, five bills for this here little trip." He came to a lavender 1980 Lincoln Continental Mark IV. "This mine. You get in the back, Marty. Mr. O'Keefe, he a paying customer, ride in front."

I fell asleep as soon as we hit the Bronx Expressway. I awoke and recognized the Hutchinson River Parkway and later, Route 684 north. At the airport, I directed Rivera to drive his car slowly around the hangar onto the tarmac but to make no sudden moves. I tried to sit up but my muscles wouldn't cooperate. Kim Woo stood by the open hangar access door, his Smith and Wesson .357 Magnum pointed at us. He evidently didn't recognize me because I was slouched down and my head was behind the door post.

"Get out and put your hands on the top of the car and don't move," he ordered. I did as he said. Billy Jean stepped out of the shadows behind a Cessna 401 with her shotgun aimed at Rivera in the driver's side seat.

"Put your hands on the steering wheel and don't move," she ordered, looking at Rivera.

"Stay cool," I said to Rivera. "These are my friends."

"Damn, Mr. O'Keefe," said Rivera. "I'd sure hate to meet your enemies!"

Chapter Twenty-Two

BILLY Jean had her shotgun in Rivera's left ear. Marty was in the back seat having hysterics and I noticed Mickey out on the flight line with his shotgun at the ready. He was surveying the area for trouble instead of watching the action in front of the hangar. That's the way good protection works. The Secret Service learned that when President Reagan was shot. In re-running the films of the incident it was determined that his security detail was watching the President instead of the surrounding crowds where the shooter was standing. The best way to infiltrate a secured area is to create a diversion. Right now I was that diversion. Kim approached the car, his gun ready.

"Good job, deputy. Are you done? I'm really tired and I'd like to sit down and maybe have a good strong drink and tell you where I've been. Want to join me?" I said, getting out of the car.

"O'Keefe? That you buddy?" He said, recognizing my voice. "Geeze, man, you are a mess and you don't smell too good. What the heck have you been doing?"

"Bill?" Billy Jean came around the car. "Is that you? What have they done to you?" tears streamed down her face. She put her arms around me and kissed my face. It hurt where she kissed me but it felt better afterwards.

"Can I move now?" asked Rivera. He was still frozen, hands on the steering wheel.

"It's cool," I said to him. "Come on out." He sat there and shook his head.

"Hey, Mister, I didn't bargain for no guns," said Rivera.

Marty was in the back seat of the car, crying and wailing. She kept yelling, "We all gonna die! We all gonna die!"

Rivera turned to her and yelled, "Shut up woman! You gonna get us kilt! Geeze!"

"Take it easy," I said. "We're in now. They were just being careful like they should have been." I turned to Kim and asked, "Is Linda here?"

"She came in during the afternoon and said you decided to stay at Newark Airport. She didn't know why. She said some man came aboard the aircraft dressed as a customs officer after she started the engines and said you decided to stay and to leave without you," Kim said.

"So they have customs working for them too," I said.

We went inside, leaving Mickey to patrol the flight line, and I told them what happened. Billy Jean said there had been no other attempts at sabotage. Mickey had the new engine on the King Air and it would be back on line by Monday morning. Jack Sullivan came up with a new schedule that would eliminate one aircraft on line so that the company's overhead was reduced. With a little overtime the trips could be flown one pilot short for the next few days, temporarily solving the problem of Tony Furman's absence. Linda and Jimmy Linn were sleeping in their beds at home and Jack was on a cot up over the office. I had a cup of hot black coffee and explained the guns for drugs business that Bolinsky seemed to be conducting.

"The part that troubles me," I said, "is the way this Pete Drurey delivers the guns for shipment like there's nothing to it. They must have more protection than we thought. Even the FBI agent in Houston, Carl Watson, didn't seem upset when I told him about the guns. He was more interested in talking to me face to face than he was in the routings, names, and addresses of the principal players. Come to think of it, when I told him about Pete Drurey, Jake Gibbons, and Morton Bolinsky, he didn't even ask about them or how to spell their names. He didn't ask me to spell Montalbo, Miguel, or Humberto either. The only name he asked me to spell was my own. He already knew the rest."

"You're probably lucky to get out of Houston in one piece," said Kim, handing a cup of coffee to Marty. Rivera declined, saying he never touched the stuff.

"I still have a lot of work to do." I turned to Rivera and asked, "What do you know about North East Financial Services?"

"Oh, wow!" he said. "That's a mean bunch of dudes there, mister. They loan sharks workin' outta some crack house up near Prospect Avenue, this side of the park ..."

"Not no more, they ain't," chirped Marty as she sat on a chair checking her hair in a mirror.

"What you say, girl? What you interruptin' me like that for? You know somethin' you ain't told me?" He hauled his hand back as if to hit her but she didn't flinch.

"Don't you be yellin' at me like that, Riv! You know better'n to threaten me. Just you be nice in front of these people. Be nice an I'll tell ya what I know," she said, standing up to him.

"So, get on with it, woman. Don't be so mysterious," he said.

"Okay, I tell ya," she said, crossing her long tawny legs. "That crack house burn down last night, jess before them Vultures got the stuffins kicked outta themselves. That house go boom, like somethin' exploded an' it burned somethin' awful. Took the whole block with it."

"How you know this?" demanded Rivera.

"Tanya! She told me. She saw it burnin' on her way by. Her john, he have a scanner radio in his car and they heard it and they do a drive by. Tanya, she say, `look out for whoever started that fire.' It gonna be hot on the streets after this if you know what I mean."

Rivera turned to me and asked, "That the place you talkin' about where they took you and tied you up?" I nodded. "You didn't say nothin' about blowin' the place up. You jess say you escaped. OH .... no! That Carlos Montalbo be on the prod lookin' for who done that and then there be that Vulture thing. All the gangs are gonna be out there on patrol. The streets won't be worth nothin' until this all blows over. We better skip town for awhile, baby." He pinched Marty's cheek. "What you think, Mister O'Keefe?"

"I don't think Carlos Montalbo will bother anyone. He's in the hospital in critical condition. The Vultures got what they wanted - a fight. They just didn't bargain for a real fight," I said.

"Mister, you gotta get outta town and keep on goin'. When the man, he hears what you done, he be all over this place," said Rivera.

"What do you think will happen if they come here?" asked Billy Jean.

"They be real sorry, lady. You guys got some big guns," he said.

"Tell me who you think the 'Man' is, Riv," I said.

"He be Morton Bolinsky, they say, but don't tell nobody I say so. This ain't so good. I jess wanted to give you a ride. I didn't bargain for no Carlos Montalbo and Morton Bolinsky," he said.

"That Mort, he ain't so scary," said Marty.

"You shut up, girl! We don't want nothin' to do with him."

"Do you know Morton Bolinsky?" I asked Marty.

"You shut up, you hear me?" Rivera yelled, raising his hand again. Marty still didn't flinch but she didn't answer my question.

"Tell me something, Rivera," I said. "How would you like a little vacation? Let's say you stay around here for awhile, out of sight, and make a little money, eat well, and rub shoulders with the high born?"

I had his attention. "What you got in mind?" he said, eyeing me suspiciously.

"We have everything you need to pass the time of day. Maybe even a free trip to Miami and a little cash; all expenses paid. What do you say?" I asked.

"You serious, Mister?" Rivera asked.

"Yes, just stay around a few days and lend a hand." Turning to Billy Jean, I asked, "When is Jimmy Linn going to Miami again?"

"Monday afternoon," she said, "but we're carrying freight, not passengers."

"We can fit a couple of living bodies in for just one trip. What do you say, Rivera?"

"Hey, that sounds great to me. Especially that free part, but I gotta tell ya, I don't have much cash on me and Miami, man, that's big bucks," he said.

"Well, we have a condo there for our pilots," Billy Jean said cautiously. "You could use that for the week so the free part still holds," she turned to me. "Right, Bill?"

"Right. I'll throw in the $500 I promised you for the ride up and an extra $1,000 just for helping out until then. That should help with clothes and the little things since you can't go back to the Bronx right now," I said.

"Now, just hold on, O'Keefe!" said Billy Jean. "This is getting expensive and we don't even know these people ..."

"It's all right. Not to worry. Rivera and Marty don't need to go back to the Bronx right now," I said. "It could be hazardous to their health and we don't want anyone talking to them while this thing is still active. If they find out that Rivera helped me, they will torture the information out of both of them. We have enough to think about without giving Morton Bolinsky any more help. Besides, Rivera and Marty are my friends," I said, looking Billy Jean straight in the eyes.

"Okay, okay! I'll do what you want. I just want this

thing to be over so we can return to normal again," she said, raising her hands.

"I wish that could happen too but your lives may never be the same. Once you've encountered people like this, your lives can never be normal again. They have that effect on everyone they touch," I said. "They're destructive and dangerous people."

"So, when do we go after them?" asked Kim.

"Soon, my son, very soon. First I need a shower and a good night's sleep," I said.

Kim had a point. We had dealt with the financial problems. We had a good idea how the guns and drugs trade was working. North East Financial Services was just a drug house in the Bronx with some heavy muscle working a loan shark act so it was time to think ahead. We had played all the themes and counter themes that the enemy had presented but it would be wise not to let them rest too long.

They knew that two weapons were missing from the shipment to Houston and they would be hurting from the loss of their Bronx drug house and the destruction of their new shipment of drugs. Their entire drugs for guns routine would now be under investigation and they would not take long to seek alternative methods of transport.

It was nearing midnight and I was exhausted. I sent Kim out to the aircraft for the two automatic pistols and he came back with one in each hand, shaking his head.

"You never cease to amaze me. These things are lethal," he said. "I can't believe you just took them."

"Where we're going, we'll need all the help we can

get. Those two weapons hold three hundred rounds between them. That's more firepower than a squad of soldiers with M-16s. Granted it's only 9mm but it's the number of shots fired at close range that counts in urban guerrilla war, not how big the bullets are," I said.

Tomorrow would be Sunday and I decided to take a leave of absence. I left the two pistols in Kim's care, took Rivera and Marty with me and went to Connie's apartment. I gave them the master bedroom and I took the couch. I tried to clean up but it took too much energy. I threw a spare sheet on the couch, took a couple of pain killers, a few aspirin, a double shot of bourbon, and fell into a deep sleep. I dreamed I was all alone, falling helplessly into a deep, dark, bottomless hole with no way out. Probably too many aspirin.

In the morning I came to and found Marty in the kitchen, the smell of food permeating the air. Bacon, onions, potatoes, eggs, pancakes, and hot steaming coffee made my mouth water and reminded me of how long it had been since I had a good meal.

"Come on, Mr O'Keefe. Marty, she do a mean breakfast. Be ready in 'bout ten minutes so get yore white tail movin'," said Rivera.

It was not as easy as it sounded, getting my ... ahh ... oooh ... ahhh in motion. Everything hurt. I wrapped my leg in plastic kitchen wrap and took a quick, hot shower. The stitches in my scalp wound itched and all the other cuts and bruises were stinging and throbbing under the hot water. It did the job, however, and when I came out I felt a lot better. I began to feel downright human after finishing breakfast. Rivera surprised me by cleaning off the table and washing the dishes while Marty dried.

"You got some place here, Mister O'Keefe," said Rivera. "How do you afford it?"

"This place belongs to a friend of mine," I said. "She's away right now so I get to use it. Welcome to corporate America. This is how the other half lives."

"Man, I could get used to this. Maybe I should move up here and do my thing in Co-Po-Rate A-Mer-I-Ca. What you think Marty, baby? Could you get used to livin' up town with these kinda digs? Huh, babe?" He slapped her playfully on the rear and she wiggled it at him like a little puppy dog and smiled.

"If you was to make an honest woman outta me, I wouldn't mind it at all," she said.

"Women! They don't never give up," he said.

"The law around here may be a bit different from the Bronx. They tend to be offended very easily by certain enterprises," I said.

"Mister, let me tell you somethin'. The law is the law no matter where you go. You jess gotta find out who and how much," he said.

"Well, you probably know more about that than I do," I said.

"Look, Mister O'Keefe," said Rivera. "You got the wrong idea about me. I ain't no big time criminal. I deal a little. I run a few girls and I take a few bets now and then but I'm a legit businessman. I ain't like Montalbo and those guys. I don't beat people an' I don't kill nobody. I deal legit with people I know and I don't hurt nobody and I don't get hurt."

"I'm sure you'll do well any place you go," I said. "I'm just trying to warn you about moving up into high society. They won't kill you or cut you up but they have other ways of persecuting a person. They can isolate you and make you feel so alone you'll want to commit suicide. If you think you can fool them by finding a loophole in the law, you can forget it because they control the law, and if they don't like what you're doing, they'll change the law just to get you."

"You make it sound complicated," said Marty. "Why can't people jess let each other alone and make do. Take you, for instance, Mister O'Keefe. You don't care what color nobody is or what me and him do. You jess said, 'Here,' and you give us your best bed and food. Now that free trip to Miami, that's somethin' else. Are you jess gonna give us a free trip and not ask us for nothin' in return?"

"I tried to explain that. If you go back to the Bronx now, the bad guys will get you. Montalbo may not be there but there are others. When they get their hands on you, they won't stop until they have what they want and then they'll kill you," I said.

"That don't make no sense," said Marty. "We done nothin' to them. They do their thing and we do ours. We don't bother them and they leave us alone. That's how it's always been."

"The rules have changed, Marty. North East Financial Services was a cover for a bigger operation involving drugs from Colombia and guns being shipped south in return. Morton Bolinsky is trying to take control of the foreign drug cartel business, specifically New York, but

I think his ambitions are greater than the local area," I said.

"That Mister Bolinsky, he's a big man round town. He take care all the pushers and dealers. You say he taken over distribution?"

"That's the story I hear," I answered.

"Old Mort, he don't scare me," said Marty. "I been to his house. Mort, he like Marty."

"Are you saying that you've been to Morton Bolinsky's house out on Long Island?" I asked, astonished.

"Baby," said Marty, "I been to Morton Bolinsky's bedroom out there on Long Island!"

Well folks, you could have knocked me over with a feather.

Chapter Twenty-Three

MY stomach felt like it had suddenly tightened to the breaking point. Had I made a mistake bringing these people into my confidence? Maybe the head wound and the whacking I took from Jake put me over the edge. If Marty was a loyal friend of Morton Bolinsky, then I was talking to the wrong people. Had I literally opened the gates and marched the Trojan horse inside the fortress walls? What was I thinking?

"Don't you go gettin' ideas, woman," Rivera snapped. "I told you about that Morton Bolinsky stuff and all them people. They poison. You crazy, girl? Don't you learn nothin?" he said, raising his hand as if to hit her.

"I learn! I ain't stupid and don't you go hittin' me!" She stood defiantly, facing him. "We got us an agreement, remember? No hittin', and don't you forget it," she said, as she poked him in the chest with her right index finger.

"I know, I know," he said as he dropped his hand and backed away, "but you jess don't forget what them people done to Carla." He turned to me and shrugged. "Women! Damn!"

"Yeah, so what's this all about?" I asked, trying to follow the logic of it all.

"Yeah man. I had this babe, Carla. She think she

know better'n me. I told her to stay away from North East Financial and all those people but she know better. She go off with that Morton Bolinsky man, and when he through with her, he give her to them animals. That Carlos, he beat her up real bad ... real bad, man." Rivera stared out the picture window and then at his feet and stopped talking. His lower lip trembled and he shook his head. "She was the prettiest girl you ever saw, but when that Montalbo got through with her, she was a mess and she ... she died ... right there in my car. I was holdin' her in my arms." He looked away, his eyes watering. "Nobody deserve to die like that."

"Montalbo did that to her?" I asked. "What did you do?"

"Yeah, well, what did I do? I went down there. I tells that Carlos, 'Look man! That Carla, she my girl. Now she no good and I want you make good on her.' You know what he says to me? He say, 'You new. You young and 'stoopid' an you don't know better, so I gonna let you off easy, but don't be goin' round shootin' your mouth off or I gonna hafta do you real good,' and then that Humberto and Miguel, they beat me up. They kick the tar outta me and toss me in the alley. Then Marty, she come and get me and take me to her place. So I don't go down there no more, an' I tell Marty, 'stay away' but she thinks she too smart. She think that Morton Bolinsky jess some nice guy john lookin' for a quickie ... yeah. Some quickie Carla got." There were tears running down his face. Marty was standing behind him, rubbing his shoulders.

"Don't worry, baby," she said. "I ain't goin' up there.

You a good man ..." she sniffed and shed a tear. "I jess wanna get back at that man for what he did to my sister."

"Wait a minute, you're saying Carla was your sister?" I asked.

"Yes, sir, half sister, and I'd kill that Carlos Montalbo if I could for what he done to her," she said.

"It was Bolinsky who did it," I said. "Carlos was just the pig that Bolinsky threw her to. It's Bolinsky you want. Besides, I already took care of Carlos. With the weapons and dope he was carrying, he should be away for a long time."

We talked for hours and I got a detailed sketch of Morton Bolinsky's estate in the Hamptons on the South Fork of Long Island. Marty, whose real name was Martina, was a very observant lady. She was at the estate twice for parties, each time with Carla. She was invited to "come back and stay anytime" by Bolinsky himself, who fancied himself a real lady-killer.

Carla made the mistake of thinking the offer was for real and became a corpse for her troubles. Rivera thought Carla might have been reaching too high, and when Bolinsky saw that she was serious about staying around permanently, he dumped her off on Montalbo, who was supposed to teach her a lesson. Marty was more than willing to go after Bolinsky but Rivera had his reservations.

"That place is wired, Mister O'Keefe. There's guard dogs and lights what go on when you walk by the place and bells go off when you ain't lookin'. Man, there's no way you gonna get in and out of there alive. Those guys, they got machine guns and bazookas and they don't give a shit who they shoot," he said.

"I'm sure you're right, but I don't care who I shoot either. You see? That's the lesson these jokers never seem to learn. They think they're the only ones with the guns," I said.

"Man oh man! This is scarin' the hell outta me. You sure you ain't some kinda James Bond 007 or something?" Rivera said.

"James Bond used a Walther PK38 which held only six rounds. I carry a Glock, which holds seventeen rounds in the magazine and one in the chamber. That's twelve shots more than he had. Besides, if we do this thing right we won't have to fire a shot, and better yet, if we have someone on the inside to let us in, Bolinsky and his goons will never know what hit them," I said.

It was noontime before we came to an agreement. Rivera finally gave in with the stipulation that he be the first one in the estate when we made our move. I cautioned him against any John Wayne moves because of Tony Furman.

"I don't know where they're holding Tony so we have to go in easy and get him out before they have a chance to kill him. At least that's my plan. Don't underestimate Bolinsky. He's moving fast and he has big ideas. He has a timetable and he must be running very close to the edge on that because he's pushing too hard and fast to acquire Furman Airways. If he hadn't tried to take over Tony Furman's business, I doubt anyone would know he's involved up to his neck in a fight for control of the drug cartels. Now he's fully exposed and he's got to know we're coming after him, but he doesn't know how and when," I said.

"So, the last thing he gonna look for is little ole Marty comin' to visit him with a bunch of gun toten' goons behind her," said Marty.

"I ain't no goon," said Rivera.

The phone rang and I found Connie on the other end. "Bill? I've been trying to find you. They said they didn't know where you were yesterday at the airport and this morning that woman, Billy Jean, wouldn't even talk to me. What's going on? I got a call from John Chusak in Chicago saying some really tough looking hoodlums came in the building the other night and roughed up one of the security guards. I told him there must have been a mistake," she said.

"It's all taken care of, just a misunderstanding, and they won't be back. I'm really sorry about it. I got tied up last night and had a problem getting back but that's all settled now. I guess things have been pretty confusing. So, how are things out there in Iowa?" I said, changing the subject.

"Oh, well, everything is okay I guess. Dad is out of danger and they moved him to a private room, so everyone is relieved and we're taking turns staying here at the hospital. Walter, you remember I told you about him, my ex-husband, well he's been around quite a lot and ... well, he's really been terrific, if you know what I mean. I'm sorry, I'm not being fair. You know there's nothing to worry about, don't you, Bill? Nothing has changed for us and I still love you. It's just that everything seems really strange right now," she said.

"Yes, sure, of course, babe." I said.

So that's about how it went. Connie's ex-husband was on the scene being Mr. Helpful and everyone was feeling good about having him around, and of course Connie was not the least bit affected by his presence. We said nice things to each other and she promised to call later. I no sooner hung up and the phone rang again. I answered it to find Linda on the line, crying.

"I just found out you got back okay and I'm crying because I'm happy. My gosh, Bill, if I'd have known what was happening, I never would have left you in Newark. Can I come over there and see you?" A feeling of despair crept over me.

"Yes, sure, but things are moving pretty fast right now, Linda. We don't have much time," I said.

She was calling from a pay phone. Linda said Billy Jean wasn't happy with the idea of her coming to see me, so Linda left the airport on the pretense of an errand and called me. She got the number from Jack. I said to come ahead and went downstairs to meet her. The guard at the front entrance of the building gave me a strange look when I told him she was with me.

"I got my orders from Miss Wilson to let you do anything you please, Mr. O'Keefe, but I gotta tell you those guys that came here the other night were not very nice," he said.

I told him I was sorry and I would probably be seeing them again soon and I would take care of their bad manners. Linda was another problem. She wasn't so easily placated.

"Oh Bill, I'm so upset about what happened I can't

even think straight," she said, hugging me. "Mom and I had the most awful fight you can imagine and I walked out on her. I've never done that to her before and now I feel terrible because of Dad and all this mess and everything and I didn't mean to hurt her."

"Maybe you can call and tell her all this later when things calm down," I suggested as we rode up in the elevator. "As for what happened at Newark Airport, it wasn't your fault. I should have seen it coming. Those fellows were well organized. They even had a man in a customs uniform to fool you."

I introduced Linda to Rivera and Marty. The two women gave each other a good once over. Rivera made a quick pass at Linda and I thought there was going to be a real blood letting, but finally Marty let it go and Linda settled down. I told Rivera that Linda was not available to become one of his girls and he apologized. All I needed was a three-way brawl between two women and a pimp from the Bronx.

"Mom is very unhappy about you and me," said Linda. "We had a terrible fight last night after I came in. She doesn't have a very high opinion of you for some reason, at least where I'm concerned. It started again this morning and that's when I walked out on her. Oh, I feel terrible but I don't know what else I can do."

"She probably just wants you to find someone your own age. Every mother wants the best for her daughter. Let's face it, Linda, I'm not a prize catch. I'm not sweet, young, tender, or trainable. Beneath this rough exterior lurks the heart of a tough, unreformed rebel who will never be tamed. Your mother knows that and she's just looking out for your welfare," I said.

"I don't think that's it," said Marty. "I saw the way that Billy Jean looked at you when we was at that airport. She's in love with you, man, and she don't want her little girl gettin' all the goodies."

"You're right about that," said Linda. "Mom looks at you like a dog looks at the moon. She's been talking about you constantly like you're some kind of action figure."

I was stunned. "You're both wrong. I like Billy Jean and I know she likes me but I haven't noticed her mooning after me as you say. She's a beautiful woman with a lot going for her but she's married and I don't intend to cross that line. Besides, I'm committed to finding her husband and that's my first priority. We can't afford to get involved in a family feud here, ladies. There are more important problems to solve, so cut the gossip and pay attention." I said.

Linda sat next to me on the couch and snuggled up. "How about me, Mister O'Keefe. Are you going to cross that line with me?"

"It's too late to ask that question, pretty lady, but there's something here that I want to make clear. We are in the middle of a war with world-class criminals and I don't need to get caught in the middle of a mother-daughter problem, so don't throw this thing up in Billy Jean's face again. The mother-daughter talk will have to wait until another time, understood?" I said.

"Normally, I don't like being told how to live my life, especially my love life, but I guess you're right. I don't want anything to hurt our chances of finding my father and bringing him back, but just remember, Bill, I know what I want and as soon as Dad is back and things return to normal, I'm going to straighten Mom out on who's running my life," she said.

"Should I take that as a warning or a promise?" I asked, the feeling of despair coming over me again.

"No ... Yes ...Oh, I don't know! Just be patient with me and everything will be just fine, okay?" she said. She set her face in a pout that lasted a few seconds before her expression broke into a grin.

"Don't analyze me. Just enjoy me," she said tickling my ribs. They hurt, but I laughed anyway.

I called Kim and he joined us. His military intelligence and combat experience would come in handy in many ways. We spent the next hour going over the layout of Morton Bolinsky's estate, developing a plan and alternatives. The North East Financial Services site in the Bronx was neutralized so we had two locations to scout: Bolinsky's estate on the South Fork and Fernandes Nurseries on the North Fork in Southold. That meant hitting two targets without either one knowing what was going on. Simultaneous attacks would normally be planned, but we didn't have the manpower or resources so it was one at a time.

"If we hit the nursery first and they manage to get word to the estate, it could be all over before it starts," I said.

"The same goes the other way around. We need to know where Tony Furman is located before we make a move, or it could become a real mess," Kim said.

"How do we find that out?" asked Linda.

"That's Marty's job," I said. "We have to find a way to get her inside and then she can call when she finds out where they're holding Tony."

"They'll search her when she goes in, so if she carries a radio it'll have to be well hidden," said Kim. "The guard dogs could be a problem. Depends on the breed, how their training and how they're handled. If the dogs run loose it may be easier to take them out than if they have handlers. They're probably locked up because of the alarms that Marty described. As for the alarms and surveillance cameras, there's always the power supply."

"They probably have a backup in a place like that," I said. "We'll have to work out some contingency plans just in case. For instance, cutting telephone lines no longer isolates a building. Everyone has a cellular phone."

So it went, brainstorming the possibilities from the scant information we had. John Chusak called to say he could find no information on Jake Gibbons and Pete Drurey. They didn't fit any of the descriptions of DEA agents currently working in the area, and of course the CIA wouldn't reveal information on their agents or contractors. I asked him to do a search on Hi-Tec and the mysterious guns.

John said Hi-Tec was a Connecticut machine tool company with a history of switching to government defense contracts when available. He wasn't surprised they could produce a weapon of the description I gave him. Nor was he surprised at the drugs for guns trade and the possibility of some government agency being somehow connected.

His last words to me were, "Be careful O'Keefe. You're up against some of the meanest, toughest most depraved criminals in the world. Don't be shy about taking them out."

"That's the same information I got from my friends in the Pentagon," said Kim, when I told him what Chusak said. "Nobody knows anything about Pete and Jake. My friends say the drug wars in Colombia are going well. They use a combination of Coast Guard, Army Reserve, and National Guard troops on a rotating basis. They feel they have the drug lords on the run and they intend to keep it that way. They say they've cut the flow of drugs into the United States and they claim to have the military advantage in Colombia. I wonder how long that will remain the case if these new automatic pistols end up in the wrong hands. We don't know how long they've been shipping them or if there are other carriers via land, sea, or air."

"This ain't soundin' too good," said Rivera. "These guys are big time boogoo."

"Don't worry," I said. "It doesn't matter how big time they are. They can only operate at a high profile level for a short time without attracting attention in this country. Bolinsky is drawing too much heat right now. Even if he has some agency protection, like the DEA, the FBI, or CIA, he won't get away with kidnapping, extortion and murder for very long. That sort of behavior may work in Colombia but not here."

"Well, that Mort, he done pretty good so far. What makes you think he can't keep doin' what he wants?" asked Rivera.

"Because he made the fatal mistake of moving uptown. The rules are different here. He ran North East Financial Services out of a crack house in the Bronx with Carlos, Humberto, and Miguel as his enforcers and nobody noticed, but when he went after the Bryn Mawr Bank and Furman Airways he stepped into a whole new world. You'd think a lawyer would understand that. Maybe he was just trying to appear legitimate, or maybe he's been breaking the law so long he doesn't know the difference. He's fully exposed and there are people who will not allow him to operate like he did in the Bronx," I said.

"We're talking about the Banking Commission, the FAA, the SEC, the FBI, not to mention the Treasury Department, which has the responsibility for regulating firearms and drugs. One of those agencies will nail him. Others will follow and before long there will be a feeding frenzy. He won't be able to pay off enough customs agents and bank managers to hide what he's doing. I've seen this sort of thing before. The government takes its time, but when it gets on someone's back, it doesn't give up. So, we need to concentrate on what's important. Our first priority is to get Tony Furman out of there before the fireworks begin," said Kim.

The two girls came walking out of the bedroom. Linda had borrowed some clothes from Marty and they were both dressed for action of a different kind: mini-skirts, spiked heels, fishnet stockings, and low cut halters.

"Here we come, baby," yelled Marty, strutting her

stuff across the living room floor. "We gonna nail ol' Mort for you!"

"How do you like it, big boy?" asked Linda, doing a bump and grind in front of me.

"What the hell do you think you're doing?" I demanded.

"I'm going with Marty. I'm going to help her nail Morton Bolinsky," Linda said.

"Like hell you are," I said, and this time the feeling of despair returned, big time.

Chapter Twenty-Four

LINDA filled out Marty's clothes very nicely. Kim Woo's eyes were popping out of his head and Rivera was salivating all over the couch.

"I don't know about this," I said, trying to remain calm.

"Are you sure you want to do this?" asked Kim, gawking at them.

"Wow," exclaimed Rivera. "You girls got some act. Let's take it on the road."

"Hold it!" I yelled. "Now this has gone too far." The two girls were still dancing and singing, strutting their stuff. "This isn't a game. Somebody could get seriously hurt," I said, but nobody was listening to me and Rivera had joined the girls as they all danced around the living room.

"Oh, can it, man!" Marty snapped as she twirled around Rivera.

"Yeah," Linda giggled. "Cool it man!" She wiggled her tush in my face and said, "I'm a big girl and I can take care of myself. When Morton sees me he's going to pass right out at my feet."

"Don't worry none, Mister O'Keefe," said Marty. "I'll take care of her. Won't nothin' happen' she can't handle and I'll see it don't."

Kim broke his trance and said, "It might not be a bad

idea to have two of them in there, Bill. Two heads are better than one."

"It's not their heads that I'm worried about. If Linda gets hurt I'll have to answer to her mother and that could be a hard lesson. Do you want to take that responsibility?" I said, looking at Kim.

"I see your point. No, I don't think I want to go up against Billy Jean. She's a tough lady, but still, if we move fast enough, there shouldn't be a problem. We just have to make sure the girls aren't in there alone too long without backup," he said.

"They shouldn't be in there at all, damn it, but we don't have any other solutions here. We have to get inside that mansion somehow and this is the only plan we seem to have that'll work unless someone has a better idea," I said, not wanting to give in.

That was the problem. I needed more than a plan. I needed an army and a pile of luck. Any element of surprise would be gone before we could exploit it if something went wrong. It was one thing to take out Carlos Montalbo when he was off guard and distracted by Billy Jean. It wasn't hard to take down a group of shooters in a line who didn't know what they were walking into, but invading Bolinsky's home turf was a step off a cliff and a long fall into oblivion.

We had yet to confirm Tony Furman's location. It was reasonable to assume Bolinsky had him, but where? I had a nagging fear that Tony might have been in the crack house where I was held prisoner in the Bronx. If that was the case and he didn't get out when it caught fire from the explosion I would never be able to live with myself. "Get hold of yourself, O'Keefe," I muttered. "It's over. Get on with it and concentrate on your next move."

I was breaking every rule of investigation. Willie Monk would be all over my case on this one. "Don't never get personally involved on no case!" he would say and of course he was right.

The Furman's were more than just clients. I was inside my friends' business, physically and emotionally involved, and I had a mother-daughter argument to prove it. Then there was my ex-father-in-law, Jack Sullivan. I brought him in for the money but he was more than just a moneyman. He was my friend and the grandfather of my three children, whom I hadn't seen much of lately.

Kim Woo was a friend. We'd been through some tight situations together. He was a member of the "brotherhood", those who had taken up the gun and been under fire. Kim had done time as an Air Force intelligence officer and his special duty assignments in Angola, Afghanistan, Nicaragua, El Salvador and Columbia made him the most stable and reliable member of this group. Finally, there were Rivera and Marty. I must have been out of my mind. I got a ride from the Bronx to White Plains in a pimp's car for $500 so what do I do? I make friends of him and his girl, take them home and give them free board and room and tell them my life's story.

"What's going on, O'Keefe?" asked a little voice in my brain.

The answer came to me as clear as crystal. Even surrounded by all my friends I was alone. Connie was gone, my children were with their mother, and Willie Monk was in the nursing home. A lot of my buddies from the past had bought the farm and I was still here, battered, bruised, and bunged up, not beaten but feeling very alone. Don Juan got tired of tilting with windmills ... well, me too, darn it! Why couldn't someone else do it for a change? Why me?

I remembered this old black and white movie where it's after the civil war and Gary Cooper hooks up with this wagon train and they're attacked by some renegades. Somebody raises a white flag for a truce and nobody stands up. Gary Cooper looks around and says, "Well, I guess that means I've gotta go out there and talk to these Indians myself," and everyone agrees. You see what I mean? I know just how Gary Cooper felt at that moment, standing there all alone.

Then I remembered my CO from Vietnam, Captain Matthew Thornton from Midland, Texas. His grandfather and great grandfather fought Indians, rustlers, drought, Mexican bandits, tornados, floods, rattlesnakes and Yankees; not necessarily in that order.

"What the hell do you think kept them going?" Captain Thornton would ask. "Pride, damn it! Don't ever forget who you are and what you're good at doing. When people forget they start feeling sorry for themselves, and that's the worst enemy of all."

So, Gary Cooper stood up and walked out into the open with all those guns pointed at him because he was a leader. He was alone and had lost everything in the war, but he had pride in what he was.

That was the question. Did I believe in what I was

doing? Did I have pride in what I was or had I just become a weak reflection of the very slime I was pretending to fight? Willie Monk used to say "When you're in the middle of a mud wrestling match, you're gonna get muddy. Don't worry about it. You can always take a bath later." Gotta hand it to Willie. He really knew his mud.

I sent Kim back to Furman Airways to tell Billy Jean and Jack Sullivan what we were planning. I sent Rivera and Marty out to purchase some odds and ends that we would need for our journey. I tried to convince Linda to go with Kim and make things right with her mother but she insisted it wasn't necessary, that she and Billy Jean were on perfectly good terms and she could better spend her time right there with me.

"I'm getting the feeling you're unhappy with me," said Linda.

"I'm not unhappy, babe. I just don't know where we're headed and I don't want anyone to get hurt. The way things are shaping up I don't think that will be possible. In Vietnam, our squad had a slogan: 'No one gets left behind'. We stuck with that through two tours of duty and we never did leave anyone behind, dead or alive."

"Why are you telling me this, Bill?" she asked.

"We're going into a situation tonight where everyone has to be alert and watch what they're doing. If one of us goes in there looking out only for number one, it could all end in disaster. This isn't a beauty contest where there's only one winner. We go in as a team and we watch out for each other. If one of us gets into trouble, then we're all in trouble. There can be no 'Me First' attitudes. Do I make myself clear?" I demanded.

"Yeah, sure, but why are you giving me this speech? Shouldn't you be talking to the others too?" She set about pouting. It looked cute but I wasn't fooled.

"Kim Woo is an experienced combat veteran. I don't have to tell him anything. Marty will look out for you and let's face it, there's no one more combat hardened than a hooker and her pimp off the streets of the Bronx. So I'm talking to you, Linda, because you think you have something to prove. I don't want to hurt your feelings but I don't want you to get hurt. Do you understand me?" She nodded her head, tears coming to her eyes. "We don't even know if you'll get inside Bolinsky's front gate but if you do, don't take any chances. No John Wayne theatrics. Do you understand?" I said, as forcefully as I could.

"Those people won't be impressed with the size of your boobs or your butt. They can buy all the bangs and boombas they want; all the sex, drugs, thrills, chills, and frills there are. Nothing impresses them except money and power and they'll destroy anybody who gets in the way. The first thing they'll do when they see you is take you down to their level, and all the little girly tricks you used in the past with those college boys won't work. When Bolinsky and his boys see something fine and beautiful they get their kicks by destroying it," I said.

"You're just trying to scare me. You don't have to be so cruel. I'm old enough to know what to do and how to stay out of trouble. You don't have to treat me like a child," she said.

She started bawling like a baby, with deep heaving

sobs, her whole being fighting for composure. She wrapped her arms around my neck and hugged me, holding on for all she was worth, and we sat on the couch like that for quite awhile until she regained control. Then she nuzzled my neck and kissed me. One thing led to another and we were getting very intense when Rivera and Marty came back.

"We'll have to continue this another time, right Bill?" she said, going to answer the door.

"Right," I said, trying to put myself back together again.

Kim returned shortly after that and we got down to some serious work.

"Two FBI agents were looking for you at the airport," said Kim. "They weren't in a very good mood. Billy Jean used her head. She told them you'd disappeared Saturday night at Newark Airport and she was very worried about it. She told them off pretty good so I was able to slip out. Everything is set and she knows what we're doing."

"What about Detective Bobby Ragan? Has he been around?" I asked.

"No, he hasn't. He mentioned something about Carlos Montalbo and going after the big boys the day after you left for Texas, and I warned him to be careful but I don't think he heard me."

We took Rivera's purchases and put them out on the kitchen table. We started with two identical zippered tote bags with extra compartments inside, one for Linda and the other for Marty. We divided the items and put one of each into both bags: a box of tissues, a bottle of alcohol, a canister of hairspray, a box of cotton balls, two sets each of panty hose (the kind in little plastic eggs), a flashlight, a box of a dozen condoms each, and a pair of scissors.

"Are you going to tell us what this is all about?" asked Linda.

"Everything here has a purpose. It's all part of your cover," I said. "I'll explain it when we go to my cottage out on Long Island."

Chapter Twenty-Five

WE had a busy schedule ahead of us and it was already late afternoon. Linda and I rode with Kim while Rivera and Marty followed in the lavender Lincoln Continental. We took the Hutchinson River Parkway to the Bronx-Whitestone Bridge, paid the toll and picked up the Cross Island Beltway to the Long Island Expressway. As we came to the Great Neck exit I signaled Kim to turn off. I'd done some life insurance sales in the area many years ago when I first worked for State Mutual. That was even before John Stanley picked me up and we went to White Plains and pounded on doors in the black tenements off Main Street, but that's another story.

I found the small variety store I was looking for and we went inside. The pay phone was still there in an old wooden booth in the far back corner near the soda fountain and ice cream freezer. A young girl was at the register but I knew that old man Rizzolli was in the back room watching TV, a shotgun next to his chair on one side and a gallon jug of Vino De Maria on the other. I briefed Marty one more time and dialed the private number Rivera had in his little black book. It rang once.

"Hello?" Morton himself answered. We were in luck.

"Hi baby, this Marty, how you doin'?" Her voice melted the wires. I put my ear next to hers and listened.

"I'm always doing fine, Marty, but I'm busy right now. What do you want?" he said, in a bored tone of voice.

There was a trace of an accent in his words. It could be discounted as a typical New Yorker's accent but there was that element of mispronunciation that always lingers when English isn't the native language.

"Hey, Mort, sweetheart, take it down, baby. I jess wanna see you, that's all. You said anytime and Rivera, he been treatin' me real bad. I'm ready to do whatever you want, baby. I even got me a friend, young thing, you gonna like her real good, man," Marty said.

I missed the next comment from Bolinsky but Marty smiled and purred into the phone in a primitive, guttural voice. It took a few more exchanges and she hung up.

"He ready. Thinks I be mad at Rivera and says come on. There be a party tonight, whoo wheee! Let's go," she said dancing around in a circle.

She strutted out the door, a working girl doing her stuff. The change was instantaneous. I bought a New York Times and a dozen Snickers bars. The TV in the back was still going as I opened the door to leave and the curtain to the back room moved so I turned and waved a friendly goodbye. A hand appeared through the curtain and returned the wave. The muzzle of a double barreled shotgun showed just below the hand and I was careful not to slam the door.

"Man! This gonna cause some fireworks tonight," said Rivera, a look of consternation on his face as we walked to his car. I gave him four candy bars and told him not to worry.

"Hey, man. Those my favorites. How'd you know?" he said.

"A leader always knows the needs of his people," I said.

Rivera gave me a sly grin and said, "You full of it man."

On the way to my cottage on the North Fork, I shared the rest of the candy bars with Kim and Linda.

"I always believe in feeding the troops before they go into battle. It bolsters their morale," I said.

"You know something, O'Keefe?" said Kim. "When we started this thing you were bringing in coffee and donuts, Chinese food, fried chicken and burger bangers with brown cows and Isaac Newton apple pies. Now that you got us hooked you feed us candy bars, not that I'm complaining mind you, they're my favorite candy bar, but what the hell happened to the Chinese food and the Isaac Newtons?"

"When this is over, Kim, I'll feed you steak and lobster with baked potatoes and a wine of your choice, but only if you stop complaining. I hate whiners," I said.

"Deal!" said Kim. "If I'd have known what complaining would get me, I would have started a long time ago."

To reach my cottage we had to continue past the Long Island Expressway, up Middle Road past Southold and Greenport. A left turn brought us home across my neighbor's potato field, through a stand of tall pines to a turnaround marking the gate to the nature preserve. My Grandfather built the cottage and it remained as part of the deal for the land when it became a Nature Resource Trust. No cars were allowed so we walked through the sand dunes to the cottage, about three hundred yards from the turnaround. Everything was as I'd left it.

"Hey, this is a neat place," said Linda. "You're full of surprises, Bill." Little did she know.

I got everyone around the kitchen table and put them to work. Then I opened my special hiding place. When Grandfather built the cottage on the side of a sand dune, he poured concrete pilings reaching up into the air. The front of the cottage rested on the top of the dune while the back was supported by the concrete pilings. He buried an old iron safe in the top of one piling next to the fireplace and covered it with flagstones and a rug. If someone wanted in to the place while I was gone they would find the front door key under the mat on the porch, but chances were they wouldn't find the safe and if they did, it would be nearly impossible for them to open it. I picked out the items I wanted and locked the safe, returned the flagstones and pulled the rug over the whole affair to hide it.

"Put your kits out on the table, ladies, and let's get to work," I said.

I gave each girl a small .25-caliber Beretta semi-automatic and showed them how to hide the gun in the bottom of the tissue boxes. Then I took the egg shaped pantyhose containers and filled half of each with C-4 plastic explosive and inserted a UHF detonator into the C-4. I activated each detonator by twisting the bottoms and lining up the two red marks, following the instructions in Chinese which came in the box. Without those marks being lined up, the things wouldn't explode.

There was a story about a major in Vietnam who wasn't popular with his troops. He insisted on carrying the detonators himself because he didn't trust anyone. Those were VHF activated. Someone activated one of the detonators and replaced it in his pocket while he was sleeping so when the remote control switch was pushed, the ones in his pocket went up as well. The major had violated one other rule that no demolition expert ever ignored. Don't carry the explosive C-4 in the same pocket with the detonators. When the dust settled, there was no more major.

I stuffed the panty hose back over the explosive and detonators to cover the bombs. Then I gave razor blades to the girls and showed them how to slit open each package of condoms. We then replaced the condoms with a flattened lump of C-4 and a small activated UHF detonator. Linda thought it was a big joke. Marty giggled but Rivera said it was a hell of a waste of good condoms. Kim said it was indeed a master's touch. I said it's always nice to work with professionals.

"So, what's the cotton balls for, Mister O'Keefe?" asked Marty.

"You use those to clean up the mess after Morton Bolinsky opens one of those condoms," said Linda, laughing.

I took a can of charcoal starter that I used for the Bar-B-Q, emptied the two bottles of rubbing alcohol and refilled them with the more volatile lighter fluid. Then I briefed the girls on the use of the items in their kits, when and where to place them and how to get the most out of each item. I had to make it very clear what I was doing.

"You have to get rid of every one of these bombs before we start. If you're carrying any of these babies on you when I push the button, you'll become part of the woodwork along with everything else that goes boom. Do I make myself perfectly clear? There's enough explosive in each one of these little packages to do permanent and terminal damage to whatever it's next to. The other thing is, don't get too near any radio transmitters. These are UHF activated detonators but a mixture of spurious VHF radio waves could set them off," I said.

"Man, this gonna cause a lot of trouble," mumbled Rivera.

"Just remember what they did to Carla," I said. "These clowns are animals and they deserve what they get."

My next task was to set up Kim Woo and myself. I had my "equipment vest", a specially designed jacket that carried a variety of items I could use to infiltrate an area. It had pockets for pliers, screwdrivers, rope, explosives, ammunition, flashlights and much more. I took it along with a tote bag into which I put my .44 Magnum and extra ammo. I checked the battery activated remote detonator transmitter and took extra batteries just in case they were needed.

"Let's go," I said. There was no turning back now. We were committed. Kim came with me and the girls went with Rivera. We would meet them later at Suffolk County Airport.

It was late in the afternoon and almost dark. The

sunset was a spectacular blood streaked red as we headed west toward Southold. The winds were shifting to the north and would be followed by clouds and rain by tomorrow night. I wasn't worried because it would be all over by then. The address for Fernandes Nurseries was on Hog Neck Bay just over the line in the town of Peconic. We took Main Road to Harbor Road and turned off at a Fernandes Nurseries sign that pointed into the woods. Rivera and the girls went ahead to East Hampton the long way through Riverhead.

We left the car on the main road and walked into the woods on the dirt road. There wasn't much to it: only a couple of greenhouses, a small cottage next to the water with a boat dock and a very fast looking cigarette style motorboat that was maybe forty feet long. We checked the house and found a light on and a man reading a newspaper at a table. A TV was blaring away in the corner of the living room.

I recognized the man as the one who had planted the bomb under the cowling of the instrument trainer in the Furman hangar, Riccardo Fernandes. He had another pair of thick glasses on and he was squinting as he read. We would see how fast he could run this time. The door was unlocked and we were on him before he even had a chance to look up, but that wasn't fast enough. He came up with a small revolver as I wrapped my arm around his neck from behind. I couldn't grab his arm and as he turned he pulled the trigger. Kim grabbed his hand and twisted it from him as the gun went off but it was too late. The bullet went into his chest and it must have penetrated the heart because he didn't last long.

"Where did he have that gun hidden?" asked Kim. "I didn't even see him pull it out."

"I didn't either. I think it may have been under the newspaper. He was too fast, even for his own good," I said.

We checked the house and found it empty except for a bed and a few belongings. A picture of a woman and five children sat on an orange crate next to the bed, under a crucifix on the wall. Riccardo's wife was a widow, a silent and innocent victim of the drug cartels' war on humanity. The greenhouses were empty except for one long box table with newly planted rows. I dug my hand down into the soil and came up with one of the strange looking roots I'd seen before. Under the table were piles of familiar boxes with SPD labels like the ones I'd seen on the airplane and in the trunk of the old Ford.

"You say this stuff is like mushroom root or something and it produces mescaline or Peyote buttons?" I asked.

"Yes, normally mushrooms are planted from a spawn or spore-like material which is microscopic but these throats or roots contain the fungal mycelia, which are the little microscopic reproductive roots or tendrils that sprout into mushrooms. This is how they grow in the wild in South America," Kim said.

"So, it looks as if they're just planning to raise this stuff here. Not even trying to hide it," I said.

"Looks that way. They don't seem to worry about being caught, do they? Like maybe they have lots of local protection. Of course, there probably aren't too many people around here who even know what this stuff is and this place is hidden back here in the woods on this little creek. Looks like they just jump into that boat, pull right out into Hog Neck Bay, go around the point and down the channel to open water. Nice little operation. Don't ignore these mushrooms either. A pound of these babies is worth thousands of dollars in New York City, and the penalties for dealing them are not as steep because they aren't considered as dangerous as cocaine or heroine," Kim said.

"I know some of the Southold police and they're good guys. I can't see them letting this operation go on. They probably don't even know it's here," I said.

Outside the greenhouse a path led down to the dock. The boat was a beauty, brand new and made for speed. The tide was out but there was still enough water at the dock to keep it off the bottom. It had a name, "Greased Lightening"; no modesty here. I noticed a pile of fresh dirt off in the trees to the left as we walked back up the path. It seemed an odd place for a pile of dirt so we investigated. At first I thought it might be a pile of mulch.

"The top of this pile has been contoured and patted down," said Kim.

"It rained only two days ago so this is fresh. I've got a real bad feeling about this," I said.

Kim found two shovels and we started digging. It didn't take long. They had buried him only a couple of feet deep.

"Damn! I hate this," said Kim. "It's the main reason I went with the sheriff's department. I've seen too many dead bodies."

"You're going to see more as long as these people stay in operation," I said.

"He looks familiar," said Kim. "Hard to tell in this light and I don't think I want to get down in there and brush off his face."

"It's Chief of Detectives Bobby Ragan," I said. "I recognize the suit and the hair."

"They killed a police officer?" said Kim, as if he couldn't believe it. "They really are dumb."

"This gets better and better," I said. "Come on, let's get out of here."

Chapter Twenty-Six

NEITHER of us spoke as we headed west along Main Road. I cut off at Mattituck and stopped at the airport, where Billy Jean was waiting for us. "You're early. I thought you would be at least another hour," she said, looking at us expectantly.

"We didn't find much to hold us up," said Kim.

"Yeah, we're sort of running with the tide, as it were," I said philosophically. She looked at me in a questioning way, and I said, "Sorry, no sign of Tony." She just nodded her head and looked away.

We were flying in a Cessna Skyhawk II, a four-place single engine plane, and the trip across the bay to East Hampton Airport took only twenty minutes. Rivera would be there in another half hour. I wasn't sure how Billy Jean would handle it when she saw how Linda was dressed so I decided to soften the blow. I told her about it, making it sound as non-threatening as possible.

"Kim tried to warn me when he called the airport," said Billy Jean, "but it really didn't make sense until now. I can see that you've been using Linda to get what you want but I'm not so easily fooled. I may have come here to give you an airplane ride but I don't believe you're doing all of this just because you care about my husband. Tony was never important to you, so why this cloak and dagger stuff with Linda and running around all over the countryside?"

"It's whatever you want it to be, Billy Jean. I'm sorry if you're worried about Linda's interest in me. I can't control that but we have to clear this up before we go any further. We're looking for Tony, your husband, and we don't have time to work on relationships right now. You're wrong about me but you'll have to wait and see for yourself. I'm not doing this for Tony or you. I'm not even doing it for Linda. I'm doing it because I don't have a choice," I said.

"You're not making sense," she said.

"Okay, it's like this. The great white hunter stands up and faces the charging bull elephant when everyone else around him is running away. He doesn't do it to prove his bravery. He doesn't do it to protect the natives or even to impress the beautiful white woman on the safari. He does it because he's what he is, the great white hunter. It doesn't matter who's involved in this thing, it's them against us, the good guys against the bad guys. If I saw Morton Bolinsky in a crowded room I would know what he was and he would know me, although we've never met, and if I could I would cut his heart out and he would do the same to me because we're mortal enemies."

"So, what does that make me?" she asked.

"You are a victim, Billy Jean. We're all victims and those are the bad guys. They don't care about us and they get their kicks out of stealing as much as they can from us. Money and power are their passwords and they never get enough. If you think I'm in this just for sexual favors and money, you're deluding yourself. I'm like the great white hunter. I do this because of what I am. Even if I have to go in there alone, I'll do it. You can take your daughter and go home if that's what you want. I don't care," I said.

We landed, and Billy Jean taxied to the corner of the apron near the fence. I got out of the airplane and walked away. I needed some fresh air and time alone before we went in.

"Wait, Bill, please." She came running after me and we walked for a while along the boundary. "You're right, but please try to understand. I've been trying to run a business and watch out for thieves and saboteurs. Tony's gone, you disappear for a while without any explanation, Kim leaves, and then my own daughter throws you up in my face and tells me she loves you and it's ... well, it's almost like I'm losing everything that's dear to me. I feel like I'm standing here all alone even though I'm surrounded by friends and my own family. I just can't take this any more. I'm not used to such a fragmented life style. I'm accustomed to more order and control over what I do."

"I can understand that, Billy Jean, but I warned you. Your life will never be the same again. Once the tiger has killed the baby, the great white hunter comes to the village, tracks the tiger down, and kills it. That doesn't bring the baby back to the mother. It just re-establishes the boundaries of the villagers' lives," I said.

"Why do you speak in stories, Bill?"

"It's safer. It gets the point across without indulging in all sorts of personalities and I-told-you-so's," I said.

We were walking along the airport boundary marked by a chain link fence. The street lamps cast a dim glow over our bodies. Being close to her brought back the powerful physical attraction that had once been ours in the past. Billy Jean turned, put her arms around me and kissed me hard on the mouth while pressing her body firmly against mine and I responded.

"No matter what happens, Mr. Great White Hunter, remember this," she said. "I loved you a lifetime ago and I love you still but we can't be together. I belong to Tony now," and she kissed me again and walked away, and man could she walk!

Rivera arrived a half hour later with the girls, and it was shortly after nine o'clock at night when we arrived at Morton Bolinsky's estate, one of the old ones built before the first world war when money was real and the robber barons didn't have to pay all those dirty, filthy taxes. The house was a Roman revival with the pillars and porches sticking out of what was basically a square granite building adorned with marble figures and surrounded by shrubbery and fountains. We got out and turned the car over to the girls. We stood in the shadows and watched from a distance as Marty and Linda went in the main gate in Rivera's lavender Lincoln. The guard called in before passing them through. An ivy covered stone wall about eight feet tall, with razor wire across the top, barred our entry.

"How are we ever going to get in there?" asked Billy Jean.

We were on the opposite side of the road from the estate, behind the shadows of some trees, and I never got the chance to answer her because a dark blue van drove up in front of us. Two men in black jumpsuits came out of the back and pointed Uzi's at us.

"Freeze! Don't move!" one yelled, and a third man got out of the front and came over, a gun in his hand. It was one of those Hi-Tec machine pistols and he pointed it right at my head. They frisked us and took our weapons.

"Get in the van, O'Keefe. The fun and games are over," he said.

We did as he said. It was a little cramped, which made it harder for them to watch us, but there was no doubt we were their prisoners. The driver waved to the guard at the gate as we went past and the thought crossed my mind that we'd been set up.

"I was right," mumbled Rivera. "Now we in big trouble for sure."

"We've got them right where we want them," said Kim, still smiling.

"Is this part of the plan?" asked Billy Jean, pushing up against me.

They drove us to a small park surrounded by woods where we were ordered out and lined up against the side of the van. The leader, a short stocky fellow with long dark hair, wearing glasses and a tan windbreaker, did the talking.

"We've been watching you muttonheads with interest, Mr. O'Keefe. I'm still not sure what you're planning but you're in over your head. I don't think you realize how deep in you are right at the moment. Are you reading me?" he said.

"I usually like to know who I'm speaking to," I countered, trying to buy time.

"It doesn't matter," said the short man. "Where you're going, you won't have to worry."

"Another shallow grave routine?" asked Kim. "The Company may not like it when they learn about what you've been doing."

"What?" The leader was obviously taken off guard. "What's that? Who are you? What's your name?" He pointed his weapon at Kim.

"Now you want my name right, Vince?" Kim said. "You never took me seriously in El Salvador, so why worry about me here?"

"Yeah, you! I know you. What's your name? Yeah ... Kim something. You were just a junior military advisor in El Salvador. You were nothing then. So, why are you here? Who are you working for this time?" he demanded.

"Just keeping an eye on things for the boys in Langley. They're going to be very upset with you over this Morton Bolinsky affair," said Kim.

"They don't care as long as they get results," said the man called Vince, "and that's what I give them. Results! Something you never seemed able to come up with, right slant eyes? Kim Woo! Now it's coming back to me. You bastard! You burned a lot of good men down there when you squealed on our operation. What the hell did you think you were down there for? You turned us in for massacring a village. Hell, man! That was war. We did what had to be done to line up the sides. That village wouldn't get in line. They were helping the other side."

"They were running a hospital for the refugees of your

lousy stupid war, Vince. They were a church-supported operation with United Nations funding meant to help the poor peasants you were driving off the land so that some high rolling generals and politicians could expand their estates and get even richer than they already were. So you wiped them out and when I reported it you blew up the hotel I was supposed to be staying in. Only, I wasn't there. They shipped me out that morning and you killed half the Red Cross legation in the country. I'm surprised you're still operating," Kim said.

"It was close but I got through it, no thanks to you. I let one of my captains take the fall. They shot him before a firing squad. Our plans were set back at least a year because of what you did. It's going to be a pleasure to even the score now." He paused and looked around, then pointed at Rivera and Billy Jean. "Watch those two," he said to his partner. "Mr. Woo? You and this life insurance salesman, O'Keefe, will please go that way." He indicated the trees with a wave of his gun. This was it. There would be no more chitchat.

We walked slowly, with Vince and another man following. There was no question what they had in mind. The trees were spaced about six feet apart so we walked side by side for maybe the next fifty feet, then they started to close in and we had to split up. It was pitch dark and hard to see so I slowed down and put my hands up in front of my face to keep the branches out of my eyes.

"Keep going," demanded short Vince. I didn't like him and I really don't like being called a life insurance salesman. I am an insurance investigator, not a damn salesman! I hate it when they call me that. It's embarrassing and demeaning.

There's something about taking your last walk in a dark forest with a brother next to you. There are cues, things that go between you without any words being spoken. Kim was trying to tell me something and I was sure I got the message. He was about four feet to my left and the man called Vince was behind him by maybe six feet. We had to bring them closer. I heard Kim suck in a deep breath, which was the signal I was waiting for and I walked into a tree, bounced back and fell into the arms of the man beside Vince.

I sensed the pivot and turn of Kim's body and the snapping arc of his leg as he back kicked Vince in the head. The man behind me did what I expected. He tried to catch me. I pushed off him, kicking backwards like a horse and caught him square in the crotch. As he bent over I slapped his gun away and chopped hard at his neck. Then I pulled the Special Forces knife and finished the job.

"You okay, Billy?" Kim's voice was shaky. I knew how he felt.

"Yeah, how about you?" I found the gun, pulled the knife from his chest and wiped the blade. He was alive but his neck was broken and he was bleeding from his mouth and nose.

"Perfect kick. He's dead. Too bad, I wanted to ask him some questions," Kim said.

We checked the bodies and left them. Kim fired two shots to make the others think the dirty deed was done and we circled back around, coming out about one hundred feet from the van. We crept up on it and saw the two guards standing, talking nonchalantly, and smoking. Billy Jean and Rivera were sitting on the ground, backs to the van, facing the woods where we were supposed to be dead. Billy Jean buried her head in her hands and began to sob. Kim crept around the front of the van and I went around the back. We hit them at the same time taking them both out without a problem. Then we stripped off their jumpsuits and put them on over our clothes.

"We thought they shot you," Billy Jean sobbed. "What happened? Where are the two men who went into the woods with you?" I just looked at her. She just didn't get it.

"Come on, help me tie these two up. We've got to get back to the estate, and fast." I took some clothesline out of my backpack and handed it to Kim.

I jumped into the driver's seat while Kim tossed the two guards into the back. I drove frantically, trying to make sense of the narrow, darkened roads. We finally came out on a familiar road and I backtracked to the estate. Both guards were awake by then but neither one would answer our questions about Tony Furman or the estate. They were pros. As we approached the gate to the estate I slipped on a pair of sunglasses and yelled back to Kim.

"We're coming to the estate. Put them out," and I heard two thwacks.

I heard the back door of the van open and close as I pulled to a stop at the gate. The guard came up to my window with a machine pistol in his hand.

"Hi, Mack," he said. "Whadaya got?"

"Delivery," I stabbed a thumb over my shoulder. "Wanna see? It ain't pretty."

"No thanks. Just had my dinner. I'll have to call up to the house. Just hold it a minute," he said, turning to go.

He started for the gatehouse but never made it. Kim hit him once and dragged the remains out of sight. Then he opened the gate and climbed in as I drove through. I dowsed the headlights and stopped behind a set of tall hedges. I took my flashlight and beamed it at the upper windows of the main house as we had previously arranged with the girls, but there was no return signal. The border lights along the edge of the driveway leading up to the front of the house cast an eerie glow on the grass as insects, attracted by the lights, circled in the gathering dampness of the night air.

"What's going on?" asked Kim. "I thought they were supposed to flash the damned light if everything was a go."

"Yeah, that was the plan, but if we weren't here to see it, they may have given up."

"So, why not just hit the switch and blow the damned place like you planned?" asked Billy Jean. "They must have placed all the charges by now."

"Can't do that. If they're still carrying those charges around it would kill them. We've got to wait," I said.

"Good grief! We're like sitting ducks out here. This plan of yours, O'Keefe, did you have a backup? You know what I mean? Linda and Marty could be dead meat in there before we even get to the front door," Kim whispered.

He was right. I had devised a simple one-way plan

but something had gone wrong. Vince and his wild card CIA dudes caught us. I still wasn't sure what we were up against but I should have been ready for some surprises. If this was a rogue CIA satellite operation with marginal sanction, being run by unscrupulous contractors like Vince, then anything could go wrong.

They would have nothing to lose by blowing away anyone who posed a threat to them. Chief of Detectives Bobby Ragan was testimony to that. Maybe he said something to someone or made an inquiry and his name got tagged at CIA headquarters in Langley. Maybe he was stupid enough to just drive up to Morton Bolinsky's estate and start his bulldog act. Whatever happened, he obviously tripped some alarms and got wasted for his troubles: another shallow grave routine. I shined my flashlight at the house. Still no results.

"We can't stay here," said Kim. "They could discover we're here at any moment." He had one of the MAK II automatic machine pistols in his hand.

"What do you propose?" I asked, scanning the area.

"Why don't I reconnoiter and see what's going on?" he said.

"Be careful, pal. The area is mined," I warned, referring to the cameras and alarms. He climbed out of the van and moved off through the tall hedges and into the shadows.

He circled some bushes, climbed a small garden wall and crawled to a window on the first floor terrace. He was moving to the next window when a siren went off. It was one of those old fashioned wailing types like the air raid sirens in World War II. Then I heard the dogs barking and saw them coming our way. Kim disappeared around the corner of the terrace toward the back of the house. Suddenly, there was a disturbance in the back of the van and a figure went running across the lawn. Then another one dove past the front of the van following the first one.

"Bill ... Oh no," yelled Billy Jean. "Both of the prisoners have escaped."

"Shit!" I said. "What else can go wrong?"

Then I saw smoke pouring out of an upstairs window. I grabbed my equipment vest and put it on, pulled the UHF remote activator switch from its pocket, pulled the antenna out, flipped the toggle test switch and waited for the green light to indicate it was armed. I held it over my head, pushed the detonator button and counted slowly, one, two, three, just like the instructions in Chinese said I should. Somewhere between two and three, the whole place lit up like a Roman candle. The plan was finally afoot but I had no idea where it was going from here.

Chapter Twenty-Seven

"**I**F all else fails, start a fire, and I'll know you're clear." That's what I told the girls before they went into the estate. I'd given them the cotton balls and the lighter fluid in the alcohol bottles and made certain each one had a book of matches. I told Billy Jean to drive around back and then I grabbed the other MAK II machine pistol and ran toward the house. I had the Glock and two extra clips strapped to my left ankle, the Special Forces knife on my right ankle and my .44 Magnum in a belt holster on the left side of the equipment vest. It was a heavy load and it slowed me down but I needed all the firepower I could get. As I ran, I could see that most of the house was engulfed in smoke, and flames were pouring out of some of the windows. Linda and Marty had done their jobs well. I just hoped they were clear when I hit the button.

Two gunmen appeared out of the smoke on the front terrace and I took them out before they even got off a shot. Each had a machine pistol. I jumped past them and found an open sliding patio door and went through it into what was once a library. There were books strewn all over the floor. A hallway led to the stairway on the left and the main entrance to the right. I took the stairs and made it to the second floor in time to catch the familiar figure of a Jake Gibbons, naked and backing out of a room. I heard the pop of a small caliber pistol and saw him flinch. He turned and saw me.

"You bastard, O'Keefe," he said as I raised my weapon. "You won't shoot me. I'm one of the good guys."

He limped toward me, slowly at first, and then lunged full force. I put a short burst into him from the machine pistol and he fell flat on his face, twitching on the oriental hallway runner. I bent down and rolled him over. He was bleeding from the mouth and nose.

"Where's Tony Furman?" I asked.

"Go to hell," he hissed through clinched teeth, and then he died.

I left him and found the open door he came out of. It was a bedroom and inside I found Marty, naked to the waist, sorting out her underwear. When she saw me she grabbed the small Beretta and aimed it my way but fortunately she recognized me.

"It's 'bout time you got here, Mister O'Keefe. I been runnin' out of excuses," she said, lowering the weapon.

"Where's Linda?" I asked.

"Don't know, man. What the hell took you so long?" she asked.

"Where's Tony Furman?" I demanded.

"Somewhere downstairs I guess. How should I know? Man, we had our hands full just tryin' to keep it together. What took you so long?" she demanded again.

I left Marty to sort out her private matters and began a check of the rooms. I had no luck until I reached the far end of the hallway where I'd seen the smoke. I heard the scream before I reached the door. It was Linda but the door was locked. I took the automatic pistol and blew away the doorknob and the surrounding wood. The door swung slowly open revealing the very scene I had dreaded the most. There, in the middle of a very large and plush bedroom, stood a naked and bleeding Morton Bolinsky, a gun in his right hand and his left arm around Linda's neck in a chokehold. Her clothes were ripped and torn so she was partially naked. She was bleeding from her mouth. How did I know it was Morton Bolinsky? I just knew.

"Let her go, Bolinsky." My voice was unusually calm. "Let her go or I'll rip your heart out!" I stepped into the smoke filled room as Kim appeared behind me.

"Put your gun down, O'Keefe, or I'll blow your little beauty's brains all over the wall. How would you like that, huh?" He laughed, hysterically.

"This isn't the movies, Mort. I'm not stupid. If I put the gun down, you'll kill us all, so go ahead. Just remember, if you shoot her, I won't have any reason to let you live," I said.

He appeared for a moment to be thinking about it and I realized at that point he was high on something, bombed out of his mind; a dope head no less. That probably explained the inconsistency of his whole plan. A stupid dope head. Kim holstered his .357 Smith and Wesson and I lowered the machine pistol. I noticed that Kim was wearing his holster a little lower than usual, like a western rig, set up for fast draw, the butt of his pistol canted outward and the nose of the holster tied around his leg by a rawhide thong. This intrigued me.

"Are you serious?" I asked Kim, nodding to his holster.

"What? Oh, sure. Learned this down in El Salvador from a rancher. You'd be amazed at how well it works," he said, smiling.

"So, do you want to take him or shall I?" I asked.

"I'd better do it. That machine pistol isn't all that accurate."

"What are you two doing? Why don't you put your guns down?" yelled Bolinsky. His hand shaking.

"Please?" Linda pleaded. She seemed in a daze. "Help me ..." she gurgled. He was choking her and there wasn't much time.

"Shut up, Bitch! You think you're really smart, don't you? Starting that fire to set off the alarms ... ha, ha, ha ... can you imagine that, fellows? She set off the alarms by starting a fire in the bathroom. Really smart! Thought I didn't have a key to the bathroom, ha, ha, ha, tried to get away from me ... stupid bitch. Tried to shoot me with a pea shooter of a pistol." He looked around the room. "What a mess," he said, becoming scattered and incoherent. Then I noticed he was bleeding badly from his left side.

"We'll leave," said Kim. "You can have her." He motioned me out the door and I started to move ahead of him.

Now, I've heard of trick shooting and fancy draw artists but that's mostly in Hollywood, and they use small caliber pistols like .22 caliber or even .32 caliber for better accuracy and to minimize damage and injury if something goes wrong. Don't misunderstand me. I'm a pretty fair shot and I've done some zany things, like shooting bottles and plates that were tossed up into the air, and shooting between my legs, and snap shooting, but that was all for fun.

This was dead serious, life or death. We were maybe twenty-five feet from Linda and Morton and he was a little fellow so there wasn't much of him showing from behind her body. I didn't want to take the chance of hitting her but Bolinsky was wired to the point where he might just kill her anyway. I backed out of the doorway and watched as Kim turned his back as if to follow me out of the room.

Our eyes locked and as he turned, he said, "If I miss, shoot me between the eyes."

It was a smooth, well-practiced move. I couldn't have done it better myself. As Kim turned his back, Morton Bolinsky pulled Linda aside in order to take aim at us. When he did, he opened himself up. Kim took one step with his left foot toward me, did a military pivot to the right all the while snaking his revolver out of the tied down holster, cocking, raising and firing all in a single, smooth greased lightening motion; one handed. He finished the maneuver standing sideways, looking back, sighting over his raised arm at the spot where the late Morton Bolinsky used to be standing.

"Darn it!" Woo said. "Missed."

"What do you mean, missed?" I said. "You got him right between the eyes."

"I was aiming for his right eye but he moved. I could have done it you know. I could have picked him off even if he was still standing behind her." Kim stood there, a puzzled look on his face. "I really could have."

"I believe you," I said.

"Yeah, they taught us to shoot from every position you can imagine. I like the going away move like that. It's smooth and unexpected." He spoke in a matter of fact manner, showing little emotion. I knew exactly what he was going through.

"Why don't you stay here and take care of Linda," I suggested, helping her to her feet. I gave her a towel to cover herself. "Are you all right, babe?" I asked.

"I ... I don't ... Oh God! I thought I was dead. I didn't know what to do. I went in the bathroom and did what you said. I started the fire ..." She was crying in great heaving sobs. "I gave him ... a ... thing, a condom. It must have exploded, like you said it would ...," sob, sob. "I heard it explode," sob, sob. "I knew then you were coming." sob, sob, cough.

"Linda! Listen to me. Where's your father? Where's Tony?"

"I don't know ..." sob, gulp, sob.

Marty and Rivera came into the room. I motioned for Marty to take over and went out the door with Kim right behind me. We went downstairs and found that the fire had spread. We didn't have much time. I went right and Kim went left. Each room had damage in it. The girls had done their work well. The place must have been beautiful at one time but it would never be that way again. Fire was everywhere, and we were running out of time and places to go. I met Kim in a back room just off the kitchen where the security monitors had been. There were three bodies in the room. One was Humberto Rada.

"I found two others in the room over there. They must have both had a condom gift package in their shirt pockets," said Kim. "Their entire chest cavities were blown away. I gotta tell you, O'Keefe, what you've done here tonight adds a whole new meaning to the phrase safe sex!"

Kim showed me the room and I had to agree with him. Both bodies were a mess but I could see the faces. Miguel Rada lay on his side beside the chair he had been sitting in. It was blown away by the bomb too. Pete Drurery was curled up beside Miguel, holding his guts in with his arms. He must not have died right away. At least the principals were accounted for. We still had to find Tony Furman and time was running out. Police and firefighters would be arriving soon and we couldn't afford to get caught. This was one shoot out at the OK Corral that I would not be able to talk my way out of.

"Let's check the basement," I said.

"I saw the stairway over there," said Kim. "Follow me."

The basement was a surprise. It had been renovated and modernized. There were the usual items like a washer, dryer, furnace, workroom with tools, storage closets, and trash cans with a handy trash bag dispenser overhead full of dark green heavy-duty plastic trash bags. Beyond was a billiards room, then an exercise room with weights and workout machines and two other rooms with locked metal doors. I tried the machine pistol on the first door but it couldn't penetrate the metal. Kim took a few shots with his .357 Magnum but the door held tight. I set some C-4 charges, used up my last two blasting caps and blew the damn thing open.

"This must be the treasury," I said, looking at the shelves full of money. "There has to be a couple zillion dollars here."

"At least that much," said Kim, "and more. Look, there are packages of drugs over here." He indicated a wall covered with shelves loaded with what appeared to be cocaine or heroine. "Enough here to supply the whole east coast for a year."

We found a key hanging outside the other door and I opened it. The room was totally dark inside but I knew someone was in there because I saw the light reflecting off his eyes. Kim found a switch outside the door and turned it on.

"Hello, Tony," I said. "We're friends. We've come to take you home." I moved very slowly toward him. His hands and feet were tied and he sat in his own excrement. He tried to hide his face from the light but I knew who he was.

Chapter Twenty-Eight

IT was definitely Tony Furman. I recognized him. He was a little older but still the same good looking man I remembered from seven years ago. He didn't say a word but his eyes started watering and he turned his head from the glare of the light. Then he began to cry. Being locked up in a room with no windows and no light, very little human contact and who knows what else; that can do a real bad number on a man. We grabbed him by the arms and walked him out. Rivera and Marty were coming down the stairs, followed by Billy Jean and Linda with her clothes on; a real family reunion. Billy Jean gave me a kiss on the cheek.

"We don't have much time folks," I said, as I urged them toward the basement stairs.

"Man, you gotta be kiddin'," whispered Rivera, standing in the door to the treasury. "This gotta be a man's lifetime dream."

"We have to get out of here, now!" I yelled. "Come on!" I grabbed Tony and started him toward the stairs. The others followed.

Kim led us out the back door and around to the front of the house, but police cars and fire trucks with flashing lights already blocked the driveway. Rivera and Marty weren't with us but there was no time to go back.

We ran across the back lawn, staying low in the shadows until we came to the stone wall surrounding the estate.

Looking back, I could see the guard dogs running loose, giving the firefighters a hard time. The police were trying to rope them without much success. I've never known any large estate to have only one entrance so I kept going along the stone wall until we came to a smaller gate, behind which there appeared to be an old stone stable. There were horsy things all around: saddles, horse blankets, bridles and horseshoes. The gate wasn't even locked.

"Can you folks walk?" I asked. "We've got quite a hike ahead of us to the airport."

"I'll take Tony," said Kim, as he picked him up and slung him over his shoulders.

It was a long way to the airport. Kim and I alternated carrying Tony slung across our shoulders. Linda and her mother did all right the first mile but they slowed down after that to the point where I began to wonder if we would ever make it. I wasn't doing too well myself what with the wounds and beatings of the last few days. Added to that was the necessity of remaining out of sight whenever a car came by. Obviously, a group of beat up, blood splattered, gun toting refugees, carrying a man across our shoulders, was an invitation for the authorities to show up. Finally, it just wasn't working any more so we stopped.

"I can't go any further," said Linda as she collapsed.

"Me either," said Billy Jean, hunkering down beside her.

I dumped Tony next to his family and looked at Kim.

He shrugged and squatted down on the grass, his back to a tree and rested like any good soldier who knew when to rest and when to fight. He remained alert, however, and so did I.

"Well, O'Keefe. You had a hell of a plan but it didn't include transportation back to the airport. Isn't a commander judged as much by the thoroughness of his plan from conception to completion as by its brilliance?" asked Kim.

"We took too long inside," I said. "We should have moved faster. You didn't have to be so dramatic about shooting Morton Bolinsky, you know. You could have just shot the SOB in the right eye like you originally planned and then it would have been all over and we could have moved on. We lost at least five minutes right there."

"Yeah, sure, blame it all on me! What about the girls? All the time they were in there and they didn't find out where Tony was. We wasted a lot of time trying to find him," Kim said.

"That's because everyone was dead. We didn't have any living prisoners to interrogate. That's not my fault," I said.

"You told us to spread all those condom things around and to plant those egg bombs in good places," Linda complained. "We did like you said. It wasn't easy, you know. Some of those jerks wanted to open those condoms right there. We had to make a lot of promises in order to keep them all happy. I slipped one in Morton's pocket but he got undressed before you set them off. It's not fair! I did what I was supposed to do, darn it!" She clung to Billy Jean and started to cry.

"Don't you think you've done about enough?" snapped Billy Jean. "Can't you see the poor girl has been through hell? We all have, for that matter. What more can you possibly ask?" she said, glaring at me.

We rested for about fifteen minutes. It was nearing midnight and we still had a lot of hard miles to go. The road was tree lined and dark, with houses set back from the road. We walked on the front lawns to avoid detection and that made it harder going. There was little traffic but I knew the police would soon be free of the disaster at Bolinsky's estate and back on patrol so we had to be careful. As I was thinking about our options I noticed two sets of headlights coming very slowly down the road.

"Look alive gang," I said. "Somebody's coming."

Everyone moaned, groaned and complained but they moved back behind a large hedge. I watched as the first vehicle, a van, approached in the light of a street lamp. I couldn't see who was driving but it looked familiar. No question about the second one, so I stood and walked out into the headlights. Rivera was driving the blue van and behind was Marty with her blond wig, driving the lavender Lincoln.

"Hey, Mister O'Keefe. Figured you be goin' this way. Marty, she say let's get the hell outta town but I say No! No way we gonna leave a friend what do us a favor like you do," said Rivera.

"How did you get out of the estate with these two vehicles?" I asked.

"The man, he told us to move 'em or lose 'em, so we jess naturally did like he say."

"Yeah," echoed Marty. "That cop say get this piece o'junk outta here right now an I say, okay officer." She feigned innocence and Rivera laughed.

"So, man, we saw you guys go out the back way and I figure you smart so we go that way too," said Rivera. "Pretty good, huh?"

We piled into the vehicles for the ride to the East Hampton Airport. Kim went with Rivera in the van and the rest of us went with Marty in the lavender Lincoln. At the airport, the Furmans said their goodbyes and left in the Cessna. Both mother and daughter kissed me. I couldn't honestly tell which one I liked better. After watching the airplane take off, Rivera walked over, handed me the keys to the van, and pointed.

"You take the van, Mister O'Keefe. Me and Marty, we goin' to Miami and get us a start in the real estate business. Maybe get married. Who knows? Careful how you drive, my man, you got a load o'gold."

I took the keys, not knowing what he meant, and went to the vehicle. The back of the van was stacked with dark green plastic trash bags all tied with a knot at the top. I untied one and found it full of money. I walked over to the lavender Lincoln where Rivera and Marty were preparing to leave. Kim stood next to the car, talking to Rivera.

"What's this all about?" I demanded, confronting Rivera.

"No problem, Mister O'Keefe. You done us a favor by gettin' Morton Bolinsky so I done you one in return," he said.

"But ... But! What ..." I was speechless.

"Don't worry, man. I took my share and filled my trunk. Left the white stuff for the police. It nothin' but trouble anyway," he said.

"Tell me something, Rivera?" I asked. "What is your real name?"

"Francis Rivera Quigley, man. Francis Quigley. Hell, with the name of Quigley I wouldn't last two minutes on the streets of the Bronx so I use my middle name, Rivera. Everybody think I'm bad because I called Rivera. Better'n getting' my ass kicked every other day," he said, laughing.

We wished them well and went to the van. I could hear Rivera and Marty laughing as the lavender Lincoln pulled out and headed down the road.

"I've got a feeling we should get out of this town and on our way to someplace else," said Kim.

"You got that right," I said, starting the engine. "Tell me, Kim, is there anything in your life you've always wanted but couldn't afford because you didn't have the money?" I asked.

"Why? What difference does it make? I am what I am," he said.

I closed my door and fastened my seatbelt. "Just get in the van. You'll see," I said, as we drove away.

Chapter Twenty-Nine

THE wound in my leg had to be stitched again and I received a lecture from the doctor about taking better care of myself. Carlos Montalbo wasn't so lucky. A variety of local and federal charges awaited him if he ever got back on his feet. One of the men we had tied up in the van was apprehended and decided to talk. He said that Jake Gibbons and Pete Drurery were CIA subcontractors who had distinguished themselves in the past by running guns into El Salvador and Nicaragua. They were chosen by Vince Mangiotti, whom we left in the woods out in the Hamptons. He helped set up the Morton Bolinsky scheme in New York.

Someone discovered that Morton Bolinsky was not a U.S. citizen and that triggered an investigation by half the government agencies in Washington, DC. It was then discovered by a bureaucrat that Bolinsky was also involved in a drugs for guns scheme and then it was determined that the raid on his estate was the result of rival drug lords competing for dominance. The cache of machine pistols was discovered in Colombia and luckily hadn't yet been distributed, but it was close; another war averted.

Two FBI agents paid a visit to me at the cottage. The day was clear, with a southwesterly wind, high wispy cirrus clouds and a rising barometer. They showed up about 10:30 in the morning, dressed in dark blue pinstriped suits, white shirts and thin dark blue neckties. By the time they reached the front porch they had sand in their shoes and sweat on their faces; served them right.

"Good morning, sir. Are you Mr. William Thackery O'Keefe?" asked the taller of the two, politely, referring to his notebook.

"In the flesh, fellows. Pull up a step and sit." I gestured to the front steps and sat in granddad's old rocker near the front door.

"Thanks, I think we'll stand ... or maybe we could go inside," said the smaller one, brushing sand off his right pant leg.

"I'm an outdoor man myself," I said. "What do you want?"

They beat around the bush for about fifteen minutes wanting to know if I was acquainted with one Jake Gibbons or Pete Drurey or if I'd talked to an agent Watson in Houston. Did I know anything about a Chief of Detectives Bobby Ragan or a Mr. Donald Long of the FAA, and if so when was the last time I'd seen either of them? I was very vague about it all and even showed them the wound on my head to prove I might have lost some of my memory but they didn't buy it and said so.

"You should think this over very carefully, Mr. O'Keefe. We'll be back," said Mr. Tall. "We can make a case against you any time we want, and we know where you live."

"You'll see us again," said Mr. Short, putting his shoe back on.

"I'm not hard to find," I countered, and they left.

Tony Furman came through it okay. Furman Airways got all their aircraft back on line and passed their yearly certification inspection. I stayed away for a while so everything could settle down. One sunny day I called Jack Sullivan and he invited me to lunch. We flew to Brattleboro and ate at a small cafe that served excellent beef tips, fried chicken and homemade apple pie.

"I did what you asked me to do with the money Kim Woo brought back from that little adventure of yours out in East Hampton," said Jack. "Kim couldn't get rid of that van load of green stuff fast enough," he said, laughing.

Our waitress was a young throwback to the sixties: long handmade dress, beads, braided hair, no bra and leather sandals. She knew Jack and she fawned all over him. He didn't seem to mind and he gave her a good tip to let her know he liked it.

"I must say, Billy, I really enjoyed owning an airline, even for a week, and it whet my appetite to be in the flying business but I guess I'll have to settle for flying my own airplane. I paid off the note on Furman Airways with the money you gave me like you wanted. I paid the burial expenses for Riccardo Fernandes and I set up the trust fund for his wife and kids in Colombia," he said.

"That was a lot of cash," I said.

"Yes. There are individual trusts for each of the children," Jack continued. "You can't imagine how complicated it was trying to find them. I finally found a missionary group that knew where Mrs. Fernandes and her children lived. It was a Church of the Brethren group and they really were very helpful. I made a donation to them, too. We should go there sometime and see what they're doing."

"It's only right that some of that money should go to the people who are being victimized by the cartels," I said.

"Yes, I agree. So, that takes care of Furman Airways and Riccardo Fernandes. Chief of Detectives Bobby Ragan was single but he was caring for his mother in a nursing home so I put a small amount aside for her. I offered Kim whatever he wanted but he refused. Said he works by the hour so I paid him $1,000 for the weekend and that was all he took for being shot at for three days; weird fellow. Money doesn't seem to motivate him," he said. Spoken like a true banker.

"Money isn't everything, Jack. Some people even live without it," I said.

"Yeah, so I hear. Don't let it get out. It could put us bankers out of business," he said.

"So, Jack, just out of curiosity, how much was left over after you paid everything off and took care of everyone?"

"One million, two hundred fifty three thousand and a few Colombian pesos. I did as you said and put it into a portfolio under one of my corporate accounts. I suppose you have a plan for its use," he said.

"Actually, I haven't given it much thought. I suppose we'll use it up somehow. I'm not like Kim Woo. I don't work by the hour and I have a tendency to get into complicated and expensive situations. Don't worry about it. We'll find a use for the money," I said.

We finished lunch and went back to the airport where Jack turned the controls of his Beechcraft Baron over to me and let me take it home. I was in another world and it showed.

"Flying is good for the soul," said Jack. "Sometimes when I'm depressed and I don't know what to do next, I'll take a few turns around some clouds and it all comes clear again. There's a clarity of purpose up here, a finality that you can find nowhere else in life."

I knew what he meant about things becoming clear. I made a couple of bounces on the landing at Mattituck Airport but got it straight in time to stop before the end of the runway. That's always important. You have to stop it before the end of the runway. Otherwise it's very embarrassing and there is a lot of paperwork to fill out. I taxied past the gate and stopped on the taxiway, left the engines running and gathered my gear.

"Before you leave," I said to Jack, "there is something I want you to do with that leftover million and a quarter. Remember Dr. John Smith of the East Side Clinic, the man who helped me out a few years ago in East Harbour? I told you all about him. Nice young fellow."

"Yes, I remember him," Jack said, checking his gauges.

"Call him up and ask him if he still needs that x-ray machine or a kidney machine or anything else. Tell him the money came from a worthy cause. It was taken from the people on the streets of New York and this is a good way to pay them back," I said.

Like Jack said, sometimes things become very clear up there in the sky.

I went to visit Willie Monk and met Saul Goldstein at the nursing home. He had some papers for us to sign for a trust fund I'd set up for my children: Timothy, Jonathan, and Samantha.

"Willie's been waiting to see you, Billy. He followed your exploits every day in the news papers and police logs when you were up in White Plains doing that airport gig," Saul said.

"I've been pretty busy but I think things have calmed down now," I said, and I told them about the whole case and how it turned out. Willie just sat there and smiled through the whole thing until I finished. Then he began to talk in his halting stutter.

"Dummy!" he said as clearly as if he'd never had a stroke. "You got in ... volved with the girl ... Dummy!" and he banged his fist.

"Yeah, I know Willie. It was a dumb thing to do but I was working undercover and I had to go along with everything that was happening," I said.

"Yeah, r-r ... right. You're s-still a dummy. Lucky they w, w ... were dummer." We had a good laugh about that and the whole afternoon went that way. It was good to have friends like Willie and Saul.

We discussed sea gulls and I told Willie that Connie had gone to Iowa to be with her father, and he began to cry. Silent tears streamed down his face but then he stopped. I wiped the tears away with a tissue and he smiled.

"It's okay," he said clearly. "She'll be back." I left there feeling better about life in general and my friends in particular. I was a lucky man in many ways.

Two weeks later, Connie called and said she was coming back to clean out her apartment. She arrived at JFK International on a Friday morning and we went to her apartment to pack up her belongings. She stayed with me at the cottage after we had shipped everything by moving van. It was a memorable weekend and I wondered if she was really leaving.

We had a heart-to-heart talk on Sunday. She said she was taking a leave of absence to help her mother with the farm while her father recuperated from his heart attack. She didn't know how long it would be, but the company would allow up to a year with return rights to her former job.

"I'm sorry about everything, Billy," she said. "I just have to do this. When I left Iowa to work for Daytime Inns, I thought I never wanted to go back but I feel different now. Dad's heart attack was devastating. He'll never work again. I just need some time to sort things through. I guess I missed the farm and my family more than I thought. Oh, I'm not doing this right at all. Please don't worry. My feelings for you haven't changed. I just need to spend some time with my family. Can you understand? I promise I'll be back and we'll be the same as always. Can you forgive me for doing this?"

"Yes, Connie, but really, there isn't anything to forgive. Besides, everyone needs to return to the flock now and then just to see how they measure up. It's no fun going it alone forever," I said, as a feeling of panic came over me.

"You mean like a sea gull? Speaking of sea gulls, how's Willie? I miss our visits with him," she said.

"I saw him yesterday and he asked for you. I think he's doing better. The new medication seems to help. He told me not to worry, that you would be back. You'll see him again," I said.

"I hope so and yes, I promise. I'll be back," she said.

We stopped at the nursing home to see Willie on Monday morning and then went on to JFK International Airport. We promised to stay in touch as we said goodbye and I watched her airplane take off. I stood alone staring out of the big picture windows watching until the plane was out of sight and then I drove home to the cottage on the dunes feeling lost and lonely.

I spent the next few days doing chores around the cottage. There were some missing shingles. The front steps needed repair, a storm window was broken, the solar collector had sprung a leak and there was firewood to be hauled, split and stacked. My leg was slow to heal but my head was all right. At least I thought it was.

It had been about a month since our Sunday night raid on Morton Bolinsky's stronghold and I was feeling the itch to do something. My boat was in dry dock and I wouldn't start work on it for two more months. I had a few small insurance jobs but nothing that needed my immediate attention, just little things like checking birth certificates, and securing copies of death certificates.

I woke up with the sun one morning, feeling like a man with no place to go and no way to get there. I cooked some bacon and eggs, washed it down with some fresh coffee but still felt out of sorts. I was washing the dishes when I heard a car door slam. Kim and Linda came across the sand dunes holding hands. I thought to myself, "What the heck! I should have seen it coming."

"Hello, Bill," Kim shook my hand. He never did that before.

"Hi, friend," said Linda. She gave me a quick peck on the lips: no passion.

"What's up, guys?" I asked, hanging up the dish towel.

"We wanted to see if you were all right," said Linda. "So, what's up with you, pal? Why haven't you been to see us? Mom and Dad want to thank you for what you did. I mean, Bill, really! You saved our lives. I can't believe you didn't come to see us!" she said, her eyes filling with tears.

"I'm sorry. Guess I was just feeling sort of weird ... well, you know what I mean. I didn't want to cause any trouble in the Furman family." I paused for a moment. "So, I guess everything has worked itself out anyway," I said, looking at the two of them.

I made more coffee and we talked. Kim had seen Rivera and said he and Marty were now married. They had gone to Miami and came back to put their personal affairs in order. They would leave again soon to live there and Rivera would make his living in the real estate business. Kim said that he went on a trip to Dallas with Linda but they slept in separate rooms and nothing happened. Linda said she had the day off and wanted to see me.

"I don't have a trip until tomorrow morning and I wanted to see you while I had the chance, Bill." she said. "I have some things to work out and I don't think you should be alone."

"Yeah, sure," I said, not knowing what she meant or what else to say. Kim got up and left the kitchen at that point, saying he would be back.

"Where's he going?" I asked.

"Kim? Oh, he's just going for a walk. You know something? That Kim is a good friend of yours. I guess I was a real pain when we were sorting out this Morton Bolinsky thing and Mom and I were at each other. When I didn't get every thing I wanted, I decided you didn't like me anymore so I turned my sights on Kim. He set me straight in a hurry. He said you were his best friend and until he knows where you and I stand he won't make a move. So here I am. Tell me what you want me to do. Bill." she said.

"I think we should become friends, Linda," I said. "Things have been crazy and it's easy to confuse excitement for love. I agree that it's not good to be alone." I told her about Connie and that I needed time to sort things out too.

Kim came back into the kitchen and joined us. "Man, it's getting cold out there. Looks like we're going to have snow for Thanksgiving," he said.

"Maybe I can explain it this way," I said, continuing. "Do you know anything about sea gulls?"

"No," said Linda, "but I guess I can learn."

"I'll bet we're going to hear it anyway," said Kim.

"Well, you see, there was this stormy day and Connie and I were visiting Willie Monk at the nursing home ..." and I told them about Willie's idea that sea gulls were no different than people. That sea gulls are the quintessential groupies of the animal kingdom and that you almost never see one alone, away from the flock.

"I suppose you're right, but what's that got to do with us? Linda asked, looking at Kim and me.

"I think I can answer that," said Kim. "Standing alone takes a lot of courage. It means you can't be controlled by a need to be with other people all the time, and to seek their approval."

"Yes, but, it's not good to be alone forever," Linda said. "It's just not natural."

"You're right," said Kim. "That's why we have friends ..."

"And family," I added.

"Okay, I think I understand what you're saying," Linda said. "That's why Connie went home, right?"

We parted friends, promising to get together later. I felt restless after Kim and Linda left and I knew what I had to do.

I called the farm in Canandaigua where I had grown up and told my Mom I'd be home tomorrow for Thanksgiving. I left the farm when I went to Vietnam as a young man because I was bored, but life wasn't boring for me any more. The war was over and I was tired of being the hero. So, I drove non-stop, arriving after midnight and found Mom sitting in her rocking chair in the kitchen waiting for me.

"Cookies and hot chocolate if you want them," she said, giving me a hug. "Better get some sleep, Billy. Dad and Jimmy start milking at 4:30. They'll expect you to help." She stepped back and looked at me. "It's good to have you home, Son. We missed you."

"It's good to be home, Mom," I said. "I missed you too."